The
DESTINY
of MINOU
MOONSHINE

Gita Ralleigh

ZEPHYR
An imprint of Head of Zeus

ISBN (HB): 9781804545478
ISBN (E): 9781804545454

Typesetting & design by Ed Pickford

Printed and bound in Great Britain by
CPI Group (UK) Ltd, Croydon CR0 4YY

Head of Zeus
5–8 Hardwick Street
London EC1R 4RG

WWW.HEADOFZEUS.COM

For Rohan and Leela

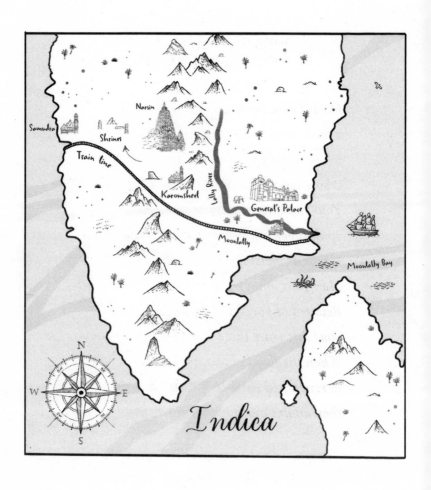

Song of the Dark Lady

Dark Lady, born of the clouded hills,
whose songs summon the rains down still,
whose third eye spears as lightning strikes,
whose powers turn back the highest tide.
Your radiance rivals the silver moon,
your anger brings tempest with monsoon.
Grant us blessings in pearls from oceans deep.
May your amber gaze heal those that weep.
Beloved of poets, weavers of words,
your soft voice tames wild elephant herds.
When the floodwaters rise at year thirteen,
to renew red earth and clothe her green,
then anoint our queendom's rightful queen.

Queen Tara, Pearl Diver

In days of old, when pearls were plentiful as pebbles on the ocean floor, Queen Tara slicked her skin with charcoal against the sharks, gripped a shucking knife between her teeth and plunged beneath the waves for so long, there were rumours she was part mermaid. The largest pearl she found was the size of a hen's egg.

From *A True History of the Queens of Moonlally*

I

By the River

One

By the River

 One

The gunshot's crack and boom woke Minou with a start. She blinked in the darkness, thinking at first she'd been dreaming. But the air was hazy with smoke and she could smell the acrid burn of gunpowder. Outside, wildfowl on the river squawked and beat their wings in alarm and a troop of monkeys shrieked noisily from the treetops. Minou yawned, pulling herself up out of her hammock and calling to her grandmother, a dark outline at the entrance to their houseboat.

'Dima? What was that noise?'

'Nothing. Go back to sleep, child.'

Minou collapsed back into her hammock. Dima had most likely scared off a crocodile again, she decided, her eyes growing heavy with the sway and dip of the water. If only she'd been awake to see, for it was a rare thing to see the great muggers in the city. She remembered the last time one of the armoured beasts had ventured this far, though she'd been tiny. She'd stood on deck, clinging to her grandmother's legs and watched its wide snout drift through black water, like a monster from an old tale. Dima had told her to cover her ears and then fired her old pistol in the air to scare it off.

Dima was Minou's adopted grandmother. She had been a foundling, an abandoned infant, discovered after the great storm thirteen years ago. Father Jacob, the Whitetown priest, had found a rowboat washed up on the muddy bank, Minou a helpless baby bawling inside. Thinking her parents had surely drowned, he'd taken her to Dima's floating shack which, though battered, had miraculously survived. The two of them had lived on the Lally River ever since.

Next morning, Minou stirred in the stifling heat. She'd overslept. Both she and Dima usually woke at dawn when the air was cool, disturbed by noisy parakeets stealing guavas from the trees. She peeled herself out of her hammock and swung down, crouching over the copper bowl of water to splash sweat from her face. Today was Sunday and there was no school. She didn't want to waste a single moment of freedom.

Minou and Dima's home, lodged like flotsam at the riverbend, was not strictly a boat or a house, and houseboat was much too grand a word for it. Dima had built it herself. The base was wooden planks, nailed together and tarred to make a deck, the roof an upturned boat, with canvas tacked over it. The wooden walls of the cabin were patched with packing cases, gaps sealed with mud, baked hard by the scorching sun. A rusted metal pipe was their chimney, and six car tyres roped to the deck kept it afloat. The shack was firmly anchored and chained to the trees, so it wouldn't be swept away by the current. On the wooden cases, a faded image of a baby, with shiny black curls, advertised: **MIGNON EVAPORATED MILK.** Mignon was the name Dima had given her and one she did not like. She preferred Minou, which she'd called herself as a baby. Her second name, Moonshine, came from the old Whitetown name for their city: Moonshine-on-the-Lally.

Minou pulled the hessian curtain aside and stepped on to the freshly scrubbed deck. Dima was sitting cross-legged, gazing peacefully over the green water and puffing at her pipe. A wreath of smoke hovered in the air. For a moment, Minou wondered if she'd dreamed the gunshot. Then she saw Dima had taken apart her ancient Hungama 19 flintlock pistol to clean it, the parts neatly arranged on a cloth before her.

'What happened last night, Dima? Did you scare off a crocodile – was it a big one?'

Her grandmother shrugged. This might have meant *yes* or *no* or simply *don't ask so many questions*.

'How come you have that old pistol, anyway?' Minou asked.

Dima sniffed. 'Tigers.'

'From when you were a postie in Rangila district?'

Dima had once been postmistress of an area of scattered villages in deepest jungle. Armed with her antique pistol and a boneshaker bicycle, she hadn't let wild dogs, snakes or the odd tiger hold up the mail once in forty years. Her grandmother nodded curtly, and took the pipe from her mouth. 'Go and eat breakfast,' she ordered. 'It's late.'

Minou sighed. She wouldn't get another word out of Dima, not until her grandmother was good and ready. And she was famished. Her stomach yowled like a stray cat. She swallowed the rice porridge that Dima had left on the iron stove and rinsed her battered metal bowl in the river, leaving it in the sun to dry.

The morning sunshine was thick and golden like melted sugar. Bright red dragonflies flitted over the deck and frogs croaked from the tall grass. Minou wiped her hands on her tunic and slipped on her sandals. The rice porridge had taken the edge off her hunger, but today was Sunday – which meant the churches of Moonlally served food after morning prayers. Dima cooked good, simple meals, but there was never quite enough for a growing girl like Minou.

'I'm off, Dima!' she called. The rusted chains that tethered their houseboat clanked and rasped as she stepped across. Dima turned her head.

'Where are you going?' she called sharply.

It was so unlike Dima to ask this, that Minou teetered and almost slipped off. Righting herself, she swivelled round on one foot.

'Church, Dima – it's Sunday. If I don't go now, I'll miss the food. Shall I bring some back for you?' Dima rarely attended church, preferring to pray at her own small altar, although she'd taken Minou when she was younger.

'Come here!'

Minou heel-toed back along the chain and sprang on to the deck. Dima's old brown face was creased with worry, like a crumpled paper bag. Minou ran to sit beside her. 'What is it, Dima? What's wrong?'

Her grandmother reached up to pull off the tin elephant she kept strung on a bootlace around her neck. She pressed it firmly into Minou's palm with her rough, gnarled fingers. 'You were too small to look after this when you came to me. Almost thirteen years ago! But you're old enough now. Keep it safe. It's all you have of your mother. If anything happens…' Dima took a long draw on her pipe, as if talking had exhausted her.

Minou examined the tin elephant, small as a baby's fist but surprisingly heavy. Dima had not let her wear it before. The amulet was black with age and the red glass beads that once studded it had fallen out. It had been tucked in her swaddling shawl when she was found – placed there by her mother.

She looked at Dima. In the silence, crickets chirred and a hoopoe made its whooping call. Her grandmother's eyes were watchful, her gaze on the huge, rusted gates that barred the way to the General's palace. In the old days, a stately procession of palace elephants would walk through the Elephant Gates into the Lally to bathe, each grey trunk holding the tail of the one in front, splashing and squirting water at passers-by. But for as long as Minou could remember, the gates had been chained up and overgrown with vines.

'If anything happens… like what, Dima?' she asked, scratching a mosquito bite on her neck. She looped the bootlace over her head, tucking the tin elephant safely beneath her tunic. 'What's going to happen?'

Her grandmother shook her head. 'Thirteen years since the last floods. The Lally's rising, the Dark Lady grows restless. This monsoon will be powerful, after so many dry years. Remember, she watches over you, child. Ever since the night you were found! If she appears to you, pay her proper respect.'

The Dark Lady was an old goddess of Moonlally, whom Dima prayed to every morning. Although Blacktowners attended church, most kept a small icon of her hidden in their homes – she was the goddess who protected their city. Dima claimed to see the Lady when she smoked her pipe on deck at night – a dark shape between flashes of lightning, eyes glowing like coals – but she'd never appeared to Minou.

Minou's stomach gave a pained growl. 'Can I go now, Dima?'

Her grandmother nodded. 'Go to Whitetown Cathedral today. Father Jacob is a good man. You can trust him if you ever need help.'

'I will, Dima. See you later!'

Without another thought to the night's events,

Minou hopped along the chains and on to the bank. She turned to wave, but Dima's attention was elsewhere. Minou followed her gaze to the vast purple balloon hovering above, its engines rumbling like thunder. The General's airship was named the *Napoleon*, though Dima called it the Eggplant because of its purple colour and shape.

Minou glanced back at Dima, who scowled and brandished her fist at the sky. She hated the General and cursed him whenever the blimp passed overhead.

'A ruler without justice loses his realm day by day!' she spat. 'Your days are numbered, tyrant!'

Minou sighed. Dima's curses had about as much effect as raindrops did upon the fat old toad who never strayed from their deck. The General remained in his palace, powerful as ever.

She twisted a ripe guava from a low tree branch that had somehow escaped the monkeys. Munching its pink flesh in three bites, she considered her choices. Whitetown Cathedral or Blacktown Church? Dima had told her to go to Whitetown, which meant cake, as Whitetown ladies prided themselves on their baking. Cinnamon wafers, pastries dipped in icing and once – her mouth watered at the memory – once she'd been given a nutmeg-dusted custard tart.

But Blacktown food was more substantial if you were hungry: rice flour pancakes stuffed with spiced potato and a cool bowl of yoghurt. Blacktown Church ladies always gave her second helpings too, pinching her arms and threatening to take her home and feed her up. Minou hurled a flat pebble across the river where it skipped, once, twice, three times, before sinking. She'd do as Dima had said – today, anyway. Whitetown it was.

Two

Minou glanced warily at the expanse of green lawn before her. She knew the mali chased away anyone who walked on the grass, but right now, he was safely up a ladder, propped against the General's larger-than-life statue. She was intrigued to see he was cleaning red paint off the General's face.

'Who threw the paint?' she called, darting boldly across.

'Never you mind!' the gardener shouted. 'Don't walk on the grass – or you'll end up like the two lads who did this!'

'What happened?'

'Police took them away. Defacing the General's statue is punishable by jail – eh, stupid bird!' He waved off a small brown sparrow that had been pecking plaster off the General's white nose.

Minou shook her head. 'Are you going to arrest the sparrow too? Who were they anyway – the kids who did it?'

'Couple of rascals – how would I know their names?' the man grumbled. 'Look – they even left a sign. Shameless!' He pointed to a chalk mark, scribbled on the statue's plinth. '*Shoo!*' He flapped his cleaning rag at the sparrow.

Minou wondered who the unlucky boys were. Had the police really carried off two children because of a splash of red paint? If you asked her, it improved the General's appearance. She paused at the huge wooden cathedral doors, listening to the organ's deep booming bass. The service had begun. She wasn't too late to sneak in at the back, but she needed to learn more. Instead, she skirted past, making for the kitchen, where bread was given to the poor on Sundays.

Minou sidled in among a motley gathering of barefoot children, beggars and drunks. Someone would know who those boys were. Minou looked much like the others, with her faded tunic and hastily plaited hair, but Father Jacob usually let her sit with the congregation, and she drew curious stares.

'Miss Minou! Did those Whitetown ladies kick you out?' Nala, the holy man, grinned at her, teeth white in his ash-smeared face. Nala lived by the river, in a dwelling even more ramshackle than Dima's houseboat.

Minou shook her head. As far as she knew, the Whitetown ladies did not object to her presence. Not that they ever spoke to her, their eyes flitting over her as if she wasn't there.

'I overslept, so I was late for service,' she told him.

'You heard the hungama last night?'

'How do you know about that?'

Nala tossed his great mane of matted locks. 'I heard the gunshot. *Pow!* Your Dima is fierce, eh?'

'And did you hear about the General's statue?'

Nala waggled his head in answer. 'Of course! Two ragamuffins painted his face bright red and ran off! And they were foolish enough to chalk their sign too – the mali showed me.' Nala leaned forward and lowered his voice. 'Your grandmother tried to help, but—'

His attention was caught by a nun, emerging from the kitchen with a basket of bread. Minou stepped clear as Nala dived for two large rolls. She waited until he'd taken a bite and begun to chew. 'Do you know who they were?'

Nala frowned and nodded at the nun, who was watching them. He stuffed the roll into his mouth and stood up, tying the other into his dhoti. 'Ask your Dima!' he whispered to Minou. 'A brave lady – she knows what happened! I must go.'

The nun folded her arms and glared at Nala's wiry figure. 'Dirty heathen!' she muttered, gathering up her white skirts as she turned to walk away.

Minou sighed. She'd missed the service, so there would be no cake for her today. She'd have made do with a bread roll, but the basket was empty. A scent of burned sugar and nutmeg drifted from the kitchen. Minou poked her head around the door to see a platter piled with custard tarts – her favourite.

She turned to scan the crowd and spotted two ragged children – a brother and sister of seven or eight. 'You two! Did you hear who threw paint on the General's statue? Did the police really take them?'

The girl stuck her tongue out at Minou and crossed her eyes. The boy, older than his sister, hesitated but slouched reluctantly towards her. 'One pagoda!'

'What?'

'Information costs! For you – one silver pagoda.'

Minou rolled her eyes. 'Do I look like I have a silver pagoda? By the Lady, I don't have a single anna!' She pointed at the kitchen doorway, struck with inspiration, 'But look – see those cakes? They taste like paradise on earth. They're meant for Whitetowners – I'll grab you a couple. *If* you tell me what you know.'

The boy looked doubtful. 'You'll get a beating if Sister catches you,' he warned.

'Ha! All she can do is give stares so evil they'd turn milk sour. She wouldn't touch me. Anyway, I won't get caught,' Minou scoffed.

She tiptoed swiftly into the kitchens. Why did Whitetowners deserve the tarts, anyway? She'd bet they ate cake for breakfast, lunch and supper too. She scooped up two caramel-topped tarts, as a shuffle of feet and murmur of voices drifted in from the congregation. The service was over.

'Mignon!' Father Jacob stood in the doorway in his long black robes, fingertips resting on the frame, like a winged shadow. His bushy eyebrows knitted together, puzzled. 'Child – what are you doing here?'

'Thieving, what else? Wicked girl!' The sour-faced nun pushed past Father Jacob to seize Minou by her left ear, twisting hard.

'Ow! Stop – I'll put them back.' Minou held the tarts out, cheeks burning. Her left ear throbbed painfully.

The nun's eyes bulged. 'Do you think I'd give those out now you've touched them? Filthy brat!' She cuffed Minou on the head and the tarts fell to the floor. 'You ought to be sent to the Home for Orphan Girls. You might learn some morals!'

'That's enough, Sister!' Father Jacob's voice echoed around the kitchen. 'Please take the remaining, er... delicacies to the congregation.'

The nun lifted the platter of tarts, shooting Minou a venomous glare. Minou scowled back, Father Jacob's warning glance stopping her from making a rude gesture.

'Father, you know I'd never take the tarts for *myself*. Two half-starved children were begging for food – come, you can ask them!' She beckoned him outside. But the children were nowhere to be seen. The remaining drunks and beggars had lurched to their feet and were shuffling away. 'Monkeys!' she whispered under her breath. 'By the Lady – they've dropped me right in it.'

Father Jacob's halo of hair blazed white in the fierce sun. His dark eyes were unreadable in his tanned and lined face.

'Please, don't tell Dima, will you, Father?'

If Dima heard Minou had stolen in church, there was no telling what she might do. Dima's bamboo cane was thick as Minou's arm and she swung it threateningly at Minou's legs when she was bad. Minou had not been beaten often but she shuddered at the memory – oh, the sting and the burning ache. *Swing! Thwack!*

'Stealing is a mortal sin, Mignon.' The old priest frowned.

'Yes, Father – I deserve to be punished – but please don't tell her.'

'What do you consider a fitting punishment?'

Minou hesitated. 'Dima makes me scrub the deck?' she tried. It would not do to mention Dima's bamboo cane.

Father Jacob nodded. 'Floors are a trial in this climate – dust and so on. Mrs Pinto, my housekeeper, takes care of all that. Come to my villa tomorrow. Pinto will find you some chores.' He raised a hand in dismissal. 'I promise not to tell your grandmother, this time. But I do wish to discuss an important matter with her. Bring her with you.'

Minou nodded, bobbing a curtsey. Father Jacob turned to greet a flock of Whitetown ladies, tottering on high sandals to their carriages and palanquins. They twirled parasols and fluttered ivory fans, as they dipped to kiss his dry old hand. Minou watched, hoping one of them might fall flat on her face – she'd seen them trip before. To her disappointment, nothing happened. She set off towards home, passing the statue of the General. The mali had cleaned off the worst of the red paint and was opening a tin of whitewash to daub over it.

What had really happened to the two boys?

Nala said to ask Dima – but Minou knew how stubborn her grandmother could be. And Dima didn't think much of Nala, anyway. 'Holy man, my foot!' she declared. 'I remember him running around in short pants.' Not that Nala, in his saffron dhoti, wore much more than that now. Besides, facing her grandmother so soon after the episode with the tarts made her nervous.

Minou had heard talk at school of the vicious Moonlally police. Two boys who'd splashed paint over the General's statue might disappear and never be seen again. She stopped, struck by a thought. Of course! Master Karu, her teacher at the Ragged School, kept open house today. Most of his pupils had nothing to eat and nowhere to go on Sundays. If two Blacktown boys were missing, Karu would know.

Three

Minou hurried through the streets, keeping to the shade of high walls that enclosed Whitetown's villas and gardens. Sweat pricked the back of her neck and the pavement seared through her thin sandals – hot enough to bake bhajis on! She stopped to drink at a water fountain, stomach rumbling. Dima's spicy potato cakes would be sizzling on the griddle. With the commotion, she'd not had so much as a bread roll. But she couldn't go home – not until she'd found out more.

As she neared the bridge leading to bustling Blacktown, a dark shadow yawned overhead. She stared up at the vast purple balloon drifting above the city, its passenger gondola suspended below. From the *Napoleon*, the villas of Whitetown would look like dolls' houses, its people like ants scurrying beneath her feet.

She darted from its shadow and ran across the bridge, skirting tradesmen queuing for the palace gates. The bridge had a causeway leading to the General's palace, built on a private island in the Lally. Dima had told her the General's servants were not allowed to leave the palace. All business had to be conducted at the gates, which explained the queue of traders lined up along the causeway and spilling on to the bridge. Huge, motionless guards flanked the distant gates, their metal armour glinting in the sun. Minou gave them a mock salute, stifling a giggle. How hot they must be in that get-up – like eggs frying in a pan!

Over the bridge, Blacktown's narrow streets were crooked as veins and jammed with food stalls and peddlers. The smells of sizzling spices and roasting corn made her insides growl like a stray dog. Dodging a bangle-seller, she decided to take a shortcut, hopping up to dart along the mud walls running between gardens. Blacktown houses were built low of wood and thatch, the red earth around them thick with fruit trees and rows of vegetables, herbs and chillies. The mud felt pleasantly cool underfoot and she could snatch a rose-apple here, a green papaya there. Most Blacktowners were indoors at this hour and besides, she was too quick to get caught.

She jumped down to wash her feet in one of the small canals that irrigated the gardens, dug because of poor rainfall. Dima often lamented that the ruby-eyed koel bird, whose cry signalled the monsoon, was rarely heard in the city these days. She blamed the General, for the Dark Lady used to bring the monsoon rains but was angered by his rule. Before him, a dynasty of queens had ruled Moonlally, until thirteen years ago when the last queen died without an heir.

'The Dark Lady was once queen herself,' Dima told her. 'Moonlally was a queendom for centuries. Even the Whitetowners didn't interfere with our traditions – until that tinpot general came along!' She sighed. 'Things were different then. The Temple of the Dark Lady in the palace was open – anyone could walk in.'

Minou dried her feet with her scarf and slipped her sandals back on. She loved hearing old tales of Moonlally from her grandmother, her pipe smoke keeping the mosquitoes away as evening settled over the river. She knew Dima would be waiting for her – it was most unlike Minou to miss a meal. She tried to dismiss this uncomfortable thought, telling herself she'd go home after speaking to Master Karu.

A lively buzz of voices came from her teacher's courtyard. Minou scaled the thatched roof of his bungalow and swung across to the big mango tree, nimble as a monkey. She settled herself on a wide branch and parted the glossy leaves, to look down into the yard where the Ragged School was held. On Sundays, Master Karu taught the martial art of kalari. Fighting skills were more useful to his students than reading and writing – most of them lived by their wits on Blacktown's streets.

A newcomer was helping her teacher today. Minou squinted curiously at the stranger. He was older than her – perhaps fifteen – tall, lean and wiry. Black hair feathered his forehead as he demonstrated the high kicks and leaps. Minou whistled through her teeth at his final sequence, as elegant as a bird in flight. Gripping the branch between her knees, she clapped loudly. Heads tilted to the mango tree.

'Someone's up there!' a boy yelled.

'A spy! Bet that's one of the General's agents!' another shouted. A crowd gathered around the foot of the tree and a hail of pebbles flew up at her, falling short.

'Hey!' Minou yelled. 'Can't you boys throw straight? It's me.'

'It's that *girl*,' an older boy grumbled.

Minou was the only girl at Master Karu's. Blacktown girls were generally home-schooled and Whitetowners sent their children to boarding schools overseas. Dima had taught her to read, write and scratch sums on a slate, but once she'd read every book in Blacktown Library, her grandmother had marched her to a surprised Master Karu.

'Are you sure this is the place for your grand-daughter? The street boys can be unruly,' Master Karu had ventured as Dima sucked on her pipe. 'You could try the Home for Orphan—'

Dima banged her cane on the ground.

'The girl will learn everything you teach her,' she'd told Karu. 'Be sure you train her in kalari fighting – like the boys!'

Master Karu had not protested further. He knew Minou was not quite like other Blacktown girls – her home was a shack on the Lally and her parents completely unknown. Dima, too, lived apart from Blacktown. She'd once had a drunkard husband but had got rid of him and worked as postmistress, which was not considered altogether respectable. Master Karu treated Minou – whom he'd nicknamed Sparrow – as one of the boys. She was his most talented kalari fighter – much to the annoyance of his other pupils.

'Sparrow! You – on a Sunday?' Her teacher took off his glasses and peered up through the branches. 'Is everything all right?'

Minou slithered swiftly down the trunk, tumbling the last stretch and landing on her behind with an explosion of dust. The boys fell about laughing until she glared them into silence. Minou was more than capable of standing up for herself.

'Yes – I'm fine, Master Karu.' she said, scrambling upright.

Her teacher smiled. 'Nice of you to drop in. Here for kalari practice?'

Minou nodded, crossing her arms over her belly to silence its loud gurgling.

'Excellent, but have you eaten lunch yet? Please, my sisters are always asking about the girl who fights like a wildcat – they'll be thrilled to meet you. After lunch, you can spar with my brother Jay here. The two of you are well-matched.'

Minou narrowed her eyes at the stranger. 'Oh, *that's* who you are!' she said. 'I almost forgot you had a brother, Master Karu.'

'I've been at school in Samudra for five years,' the boy answered. 'I remember you, though – a tiny thing who looked like butter wouldn't melt to ghee in her mouth!'

Minou drew herself up and gave him a withering look she'd learned from Dima. '*Samudra?* Why, wasn't this place good enough for you? Only Whitetowners send their kids away – how come they got rid of you?'

The boy grinned at her. 'You ask a lot of questions. When did they make you chief of police?'

'Stop it, you two – let Sparrow eat and you can catch up later. You should see her fight, Jay.' Master Karu slapped his brother on the back. 'Wings on her feet and a punch like a thunderclap! Sparrow, this way.'

Her teacher waved her inside. Sliding off her dusty sandals, Minou followed him into the cool bungalow, which smelled of sandalwood and camphor. She hadn't met Karu's sisters, not properly. His widowed mother was strict, so the girls remained black-clad, veiled figures, carrying trays of lemonade or mango slices out for the schoolchildren. The thatched wooden building was built in the old Moonlally style, with pearly shell-panelled windows, so she'd never even peeked inside.

Karu opened the door to a dim room, lit by oil lamps that spilled yellow over a tiled floor. Shadows flickered on the walls and four faces took shape in the gloom. Karu's mother and sisters were seated on the ground, sewing. Minou stared in wonder at the gleaming gold silk draped over their laps, a pattern of red cherries growing with each flash of their silver needles. In Moonlally, even wealthy Whitetowners wore white and Blacktowners black.

She could not imagine who this extravagant creation was for.

Four

'This is Sparrow – my pupil. Ma, could you find her some lunch?'

Karu's mother looked up and smiled as she bit off a thread. 'Welcome, dear. Girls! Who's going to take Sparrow into the kitchen and feed her?'

The three sisters put aside their embroidery and scrambled up.

'I'll take her!'

'No, me!' Their voices rang out like a peal of church bells.

'You may all go,' Karu's mother agreed.

Minou followed the clink of anklets and rustle of silk tunics down the passage to the kitchen. Karu's sisters chattered away, pleased to have a distraction from work.

'I'm Darina, the eldest!'

'Meena – I'm next.'

'And I'm Leena, the littlest.'

'Is Sparrow your real name?' Darina asked.

Minou shook her head.

'Honestly! Karu gives everyone silly nicknames – it's embarrassing. What's your real name?'

'Mignon Moonshine. But people call me Minou.'

'But Mignon's so pretty!' Leena gasped. 'Do you like papaya?'

Minou was given a bowl of scented water to wash her hands and seated upon a low stool. A metal dish of steaming rice, lentils, curds and papaya sprinkled with salt and lime was placed before her. She ate hungrily, pausing only to ask,

'The cloth you're embroidering – who's it for? I've never seen anything like it!'

'The gold silk? Why, the General's daughter, of course! One of the many robes for Miss Ophelia's wedding finery.' Darina rolled her eyes at a painting of the General on the wall.

The General's chalk-white face glowered at them. He was seated on a huge mechanical elephant of gleaming wood and brass, dressed in his gold-buttoned military uniform. By law, every home in Moonlally was required to hang a portrait of the General. Dima had turned theirs to face the wall of their shack.

'I've never seen that wooden elephant before,' Minou remarked.

'Moonlally's Magnificent Mechanical Elephant? Hasn't Karu told you the story?' Darina sounded surprised.

'Let's tell her!' Leena piped.

'Well,' Darina began. 'Wait – let's see what my brother's taught you. Have you heard of the old queen – who ruled Moonlally before the General came to power?'

Minou nodded. 'The General is the old queen's nephew – is that right?'

'Yes. When she died, the young queen, her daughter, was barely sixteen. The Commandant decided Moonlally needed a different ruler. He knew the General would allow Whitetowners to do what they wanted – mine the land, build factories, cut down forests—'

'And the young queen? I heard she died...'

Darina shook her head. 'Poor girl. The General and Commandant locked her up, until she pined to death.'

'But how could they do such a thing?'

'The General's mad in the head! And the Commandant uses him to get what he wants. Indirect rule, they call it. But we've seen the puppet show, we know who pulls the strings!'

'Get back to the *elephant!*' Meena complained.

'Well, after the poor young queen was locked up, the Commandant arranged for his sister to marry the General. Naturally, the General wanted to impress his bride. He ordered the palace clockmaker to build a mechanical elephant to ride upon at the wedding. *Elephantus Conculcaverit!* "The Elephant Trampled" – that's his motto!'

Darina puffed out her chest and twirled an imaginary moustache in imitation of the General. 'Now, Shri

– the palace clockmaker – was the greatest craftsman in Moonlally. He invented something new every week! He made marvellous toys for the young queen—'

'Jewelled birds that flew and golden bees that buzzed!' Leena put in.

'But he'd never attempted anything the size of an elephant. He worked on it for months. Carved from mahogany, with brass joints and a leather trunk and ears. On his wedding day, the General climbed on, his servants cranked the wind-up tail and Moonlally's Magnificent Mechanical Elephant rolled across the palace grounds!' Darina shot Minou a sly glance.

'What happened next?' she asked, as Karu's sisters giggled.

'Well, Shri had always made *small* mechanicals,' Darina explained. 'Birds and butterflies that flitted through the air until their clockwork ran down. But they'd wound the elephant up too far! It rolled past the wedding tent, out of the Elephant Gates and into—'

'The river!' added Leena with glee.

'Yes! Right into the water, the General clinging to its back! And it stayed there, deep in the mud, until a tractor pulled it out. That portrait,' she nodded at the wall, 'was painted for his wedding. No one dared show it to the General after that fiasco. Our mother's the palace dressmaker, so she took it home.'

'But that's not the whole story.' Minou turned at Jay's voice. He leaned against the doorway, arms folded. 'Tell her, Darina. What the General did to the old clockmaker, afterwards.'

Darina picked Minou's bowl up. 'Don't start, Jay.'

'Start what?'

'I hate the General as much as you – but we don't have to dwell on every terrible thing he's done.' She stacked the dishes together with a clatter.

'I didn't ask you to,' Jay replied. 'I want to do something about him. To fight him – together.'

'And Mother? You'll send her to an early grave – you know how she worries!' Darina smiled at Minou. 'Don't mind us. You're lucky not to have brothers, Mignon.' She clapped her hands, chiding, 'Back to work, girls!'

Jay nodded at the courtyard. 'Karu wants to see us sparring,' he told Minou.

'But I want to watch Sparrow fight!' Leena demanded.

Darina shook her head. 'Fighting's not for girls – Mignon's different! Besides, Miss Ophelia's clothes must be ready for the wedding. Eleven dresses, Mignon, each to be made twice! Our fingers will have fallen off by the big day.'

'Two ballgowns, one of gold tussore with real rubies!' Meena sang.

'The second of gold silk, with red crystal beads.' Darina echoed. The sisters left the kitchen, their anklet chimes fading as they disappeared down the shadowy corridor. Leena turned to mouth, 'Good luck!' at Minou, who smiled back. She liked Karu's sisters. As for Jay, she wasn't sure about him yet.

The tall boy stood in the courtyard, shielding his eyes against the sun's glare. Minou faced him.

'So, tell me,' she challenged. 'What happened to the clockmaker?'

Jay's black eyes clouded. 'Sorry – I shouldn't have barged in like that. It was rude.'

She shrugged. 'I don't care about manners – I want the truth.'

The boy grimaced. 'Sure you can take it?'

'Try me.'

Jay sighed. 'The General had the clockmaker's right hand cut off at the wrist. So he'd never make anything again.'

Minou swallowed, her mouth dry as ashes. Everyone knew the General was cruel – but to cut off a craftsman's right hand? How could anyone be so vicious? She felt sick. 'Is that really true?' she whispered.

Jay nodded, his face serious. 'That's why I can't sit around doing nothing,' he told her. 'Let's move under the tree – it's cooler.'

Minou followed him into the deep shade beneath the mango tree, its leaves stirring in a weary breeze. She felt suddenly dizzy, the dusty earth tilting under her. Glancing up, she saw the boys forming a circle around them. A few faces were missing, but it was Sunday, not a school day, so that was expected. Master Karu approached to signal they should begin.

'Warm-up and first series, please.'

Minou tightened her scarf about her waist and tried to steady her mind. She couldn't let her teacher down – not when he'd told Jay how good a fighter she was. She drove her feet into the ground, taking deep breaths until she felt better. They worked through the warm-up sequence, then stances, followed by lunges, kicks and punches. Master Karu nodded his approval. 'Second series with elevations!'

Minou glanced at Jay as they practised, sizing up her opponent. High kicks and flying lunges were her strength. She lacked power but her reflexes were quick, leaps high and landings precise.

'Eagle in flight! Crouching panther!' Karu called as they whirled through their positions. The tin elephant bumped against her breastbone as she vaulted the air. She remembered, with a pang, that Dima would be worried about her by now.

'Tired?' Karu asked.

Minou shook her head. She never felt tired when fighting. Her mind was alert, her body humming with energy. Kalari made her fearless, her black shadow soaring under her with a life of its own. Karu often joked that she was the daughter of the wind, like the monkey god of the old tales.

'Sparring. Are you both ready?'

'Ready.' Minou wiped the sweat from her forehead and turned to Jay. They bowed to each other, hands folded, and took three steps backwards.

Jay was the best opponent she'd sparred against, but Minou wasn't worried. The boys yelled encouragement as she circled him, changing direction swiftly. Jay was taller and stronger than her, but also heavier – if she caught him off-balance, she could use his weight against him. She let fly a high kick he deflected, following with a double twist and swivel punch. Jay came back with a half-hearted lunge that she ducked easily, landing smartly on one foot.

Minou smirked. 'What was *that*?' she taunted.

'Etiquette!' Karu warned. Addressing your opponent during a bout was forbidden.

Jay pressed his lips together. Minou wasn't sure if he was cross or trying not to laugh. His next kick was powerful but she dodged it, spinning, and stung him with a blow to his shoulder. The boy's balance faltered, and Minou saw him wince. They stalked each other, neither giving way, Jay's face tight with concentration. He launched three high kicks, one after another. The first caught Minou's hip – she sprang so the second grazed her, cartwheeled to miss the third and launched a powerful flying kick, her foot meeting his chest. The older boy's leg was caught mid-air, his other foot slipped from under him and a second later he was sprawled on his back in the dust.

Karu tried to hide his laughter as he helped his brother on to his feet. 'More than you bargained for, eh? She might be small – but she's fierce!'

'I'm not used to sparring with someone so short. My balance is off!' Jay grumbled. The boy raised his hands to Minou in surrender. 'You're a good fighter. Power, coordination and those kicks! Thanks for destroying my reputation in Moonlally. I've been home a week.'

The other boys were straggling off, shaking their heads in dismay. Minou smiled, satisfied she'd shown them. At least Karu's brother was a good loser. 'I'm happy to go a second round – give you a chance to recover your reputation?'

'Not today, Sparrow,' Karu sighed. 'I need to look for Tal and Little. They weren't in school yesterday. You haven't seen them?'

'Tal and Little are missing?' Minou clapped her hands over her mouth. 'By the Lady! I forgot. Master Karu – that's why I came.' She told him what she'd learned at Whitetown Cathedral.

He shook his head. 'Defacing a statue of the General is a serious matter. Why would they do something so stupid?'

Minou shrugged. Like all the Ragged School boys, Tal and Little ran wild as monkeys and were always up to some prank or other.

Her teacher frowned. 'I'll speak to an attorney. The General's police are like scorpions – once they see you, you're as good as done for. But even they can't arrest two minors without charges.'

'I wouldn't bet on that, brother. They're capable of anything.' Jay kicked up the courtyard dust, red under the setting sun.

Sunset! Minou glanced at the crimson light over Blacktown's low roofs. Dima would be fretting – it was almost suppertime. She was in big trouble. Bobbing a quick curtsey, she hopped on to the courtyard wall,

'I must go – I'm late! Please thank your mother for lunch, Master Karu. See you around,' she added to Jay.

Five

Minou took her familiar zigzag route through Blacktown, flitting across gardens and scaling low rooftops. This way, she'd make it home before nightfall.

The evening sky had softened to violet as she reached the bridge over the Lally. Crossing the river, she saw the line of tradesmen queuing at the palace gates had dispersed. The armoured guards stood lifeless as statues. In the distance a grey plume of smoke drifted. Had there been a fire somewhere? But that didn't explain why the bridge was deserted, except for a crow, pecking at a mango skin. Scurrying on, she noticed the stench of smoke grew stronger. Whitetown fanned out before her, its elegant villas shuttered and wide avenues silent, empty of the grand carriages usually out in the cool evening air. Where was everyone? A hurry of footsteps sounded behind her and she whirled round, fists raised.

'You again!'

Jay winked at her. 'Took me ages to find you. Where did you disappear to?'

Minou shrugged. 'I took a shortcut across town. What's up?'

'There's been an explosion on the *Napoleon*. The police are treating it as an attempt on the General's life.'

'So?' Minou was unmoved. This wasn't the first time – rebels had derailed the royal train only last year.

'Thought I'd better check you were all right. There's a curfew in Blacktown – police are rounding up anyone out on the streets. Karu was worried – especially after what happened to Tal and Little.'

A black carriage hurtled past, its horses at full trot and its flag bearing a white rose. Minou glanced at the lace-curtained window and saw a girl about her age, white-gloved fingers pressed to the glass. The girl stared back. Minou would have made a face at her, but thought this unwise.

'Maybe we'd better walk by the river?' She pointed to the flight of rickety wooden steps leading to the water below. If they stayed on the towpath, no one could see them from the road. 'That was the Commandant of Whitetown's carriage,' Jay said in a low voice as he followed her down. 'Good idea to keep out of sight.' But if that was the Commandant's carriage, who was the girl? Perhaps his daughter, Minou wondered.

Shooting a sidelong glance at Jay, she decided he wasn't so different from the boys at school, even if he had lived in the big city of Samudra. She'd speak to him as if he was one of her schoolmates.

'Why did you follow me, Jay?'

'To apologise. You and I got off on the wrong foot. I argued with my sisters and interrupted your lunch, then—'

'Then I knocked you flat,' Minou reminded him.

Jay laughed. 'You did. Anyway – with the curfew – I thought I'd make up by escorting you home.'

Minou snorted. 'You did learn some fine manners in Samudra. So why were you really sent away?'

Jay kicked at a coconut husk on the dusty ground. 'I won a scholarship to the School of Navigation. I'm good with numbers. Also, Ma wanted me away from Moonlally. She was worried about the company I kept.'

'What kind of company?'

Jay frowned. 'The kind that doesn't like the General. Tell me – what did you see at the cathedral?'

Minou shrugged. 'Tal and Little – if it was them – had thrown red paint on that ugly statue of the General. They chalked a picture on the base.'

'Was it a flower? Like this.' Jay bent to the ground and held out a wisp of stem with three lime petals.

Minou stared at the green orchid. The tiny wildflowers grew by the Lally, opening at dusk with a delicate fragrance. The Green Orchids were also a band of Blacktown rebels, fighting the General. The flower was their symbol – she'd seen it painted on walls and chalked on flagstones. She'd even heard that rebel leaders tattooed it on their left arm.

'I didn't see it properly. It was half-rubbed off.' She looked curiously at Jay's arms, covered by the sleeves of his black tunic. Could he be a rebel? He wasn't much older than her. 'Is *that* why you followed me?' she asked accusingly. The towpath was silent, except for the rush of the current and clamour of evening birdsong. She lowered her voice to a whisper. 'To recruit me for the... rebels.'

Jay nodded. 'I know a fighter when I see one – and you're a fighter, Sparrow. We could do with someone like you.'

'Me, a Green Orchid? By the Lady – I can't fire a gun, much less blow anything up.'

'Lots of kids at Karu's school help. They deliver messages or keep lookout. Ask your grandmother – she's one of us.'

'Dima!' Minou gasped. '*Really?*' Her grandmother, a Green Orchid? Dima barely left the shack except to collect her pension. 'Is that why the police took Tal and Little – because they're Green Orchids?' she asked. If the police knew the boys were rebels, their punishment would be harsh.

Jay sighed. 'I hope not. Karu's dealing with it. With luck, they'll be out soon.'

Minou frowned, remembering last night's gunshot. Had Dima fired at a crocodile – or something else? 'Look, you should go, Jay. Maybe Samudra girls like to be walked home, but I know my way around Moonlally. This is my city.'

The boy nodded. 'All right. I've got a busy day

tomorrow, anyway. Need to look for work. I'm a trained navigator, but round here I'll have to take what I can get.'

'What does a navigator actually do – read maps?'

'Map reading and other navigational arts – everything from kamal and sextant to compass and radar. Mostly ships, but I've worked on airships and planes too.' He spread his arms wide. 'I'd like to be a pilot, one day. The skies are the future.'

'Not for the *Napoleon* – that just blew up!' Minou scoffed.

Jay's eyes sparked in the fading light. 'What's more deadly – a cobra or a wild dog?'

She frowned at him. 'Um… a cobra, stupid? You really were in the big city too long.'

The boy grinned. 'But why? Because you hear a pack of dogs way off,' he told her. 'A cobra's silent. You don't know it's there until it strikes – and then, it's deadly.'

Minou nodded, though she wasn't entirely sure what he meant. 'Jay – ' she lowered her voice 'do you think the General's dead?'

Jay shook his head, his face hard. 'I'll bet the General wasn't on that airship. I know the crew escaped – saw them paraglide off. But he's not indestructible. His days are numbered, ask your grandmother! I know she wants to protect you, but you're old enough to know the truth. Think about it.'

Minou touched the tin elephant, tucked beneath her tunic. *You're old enough now,* Dima had said, before she'd given it to her that morning. She nodded. 'I'll talk to Dima,' she told him.

Jay raised a hand, 'You know where to find me.' He swivelled on his heels and strode away. She watched him vanish into the shadows and then walked on. A light breeze stirred the water's surface, bats swooped low in the twilight sky. Could a ragtag bunch of kids – if they made up the Green Orchids – really bring down the powerful General? Dima would be on deck by now, smoking her evening pipe. She'd brandish her bamboo cane at Minou for being so late. But once she'd calmed down, Dima would tell her what to do about the rebels. She always had an opinion, even if she only expressed it with a firm shake of her grey head. Minou knew her grandmother would like Jay. Next time, she'd let him walk her home.

She made her way towards their houseboat, bobbing on the black water. Why couldn't she see smoke curling from the metal chimney? And why hadn't Dima lit the lantern? At night, with its warm amber glow, their tumbledown shack looked almost cosy. She stopped in her tracks when she saw the chain. Drifting loosely on the surface, it was one of four that tethered their floating home to the trees.

It had been cut through.

Minou's heart bumped at her collarbone. Jittery with fear, she leaped across the two-metre gap between boat and bank, darted across the deck and tore away the hessian curtain. Her eyes adjusted to the gloom. Charcoal from the fire littered the floor, a copper pot rolled with the river's swell and Dima's clay icon of the Dark Lady lay shattered. A stink of gunpowder and an iron taint of blood hung in the air.

Her breath flew from her. Dima lay on the floor, the old pistol beside her.

Minou's legs buckled. She sank with a shocked cry, clasped her grandmother's shoulders and pressed an ear to Dima's chest. Halting her own ragged breathing, she listened. *Nothing.* She couldn't hear the deep, comforting thud of Dima's heartbeat. She reached to touch Dima's face and felt a stickiness on her cheek. And then she saw it – scorched skin around a gaping hole at the temple. A dull cry tore from her.

Dima was dead. Shot in the head with her own pistol.

Minou curled beside her grandmother, sobbing helplessly. Through the open doorway, clouds rolled across a purple sky. Rain spat at the roof; an unsettled wind rocked the shack like a cradle. Hours passed. Minou must have cried herself to sleep, for when she woke, the squall was over and the waters were calm.

She stood, stiff and heartsore, and found a blanket to cover her grandmother, tenderly closing Dima's eyes. Picking up the broom, she swept up the scattered charcoal and fragments of clay. The General's white face scowled from his portrait on the wall.

Out on deck, she crouched to wash her hands in the river. The night was warm and clear, the moon a blind eye staring down at her. She wiped her hands on her tunic. Who could have killed Dima? And why? Hot tears spilled as she hugged her knees tight to stop herself shaking.

'I'll find whoever did this, Dima – see if I don't. By the Lady, they'll be sorry they were born,' she whispered. The wind stirred the trees, leaves rustling as if in answer.

A faint scent of rain on dry earth blew across the Lally. Under the moonlight, shadows swayed. She had the impression of someone moving on the opposite bank; an inky shape drifting before the vines of the Elephant Gates. But that was impossible. The rusted gates were chained up, beyond them lay only an abandoned corner of the vast palace grounds.

'Go away!' she shouted. 'I've got a gun here and I'll use it!'

The figure faded into nothing – a trick of the moonlight. Minou's heart thudded against her ribcage; the tin amulet Dima had given her warm against her throat. She pressed the small elephant to her lips. She'd never felt alone at night before. Her grandmother had always been there, with her comforting smell of pipe smoke.

Now, Minou had to take care of her in return.

Dima had given instructions for her funeral. She'd asked to be laid to rest in her family tomb at Blacktown Cemetery. There was to be a full ceremony – candles lit, palm wine drunk and a poet to sing funeral songs at her grave.

'But that's not going to happen for a long time, Dima,' Minou had said. She remembered how she'd pressed herself into Dima's side, resting her cheek against her shoulder.

'No,' Dima had agreed. 'Not for a long time.'

Six

Minou lifted her head and blinked. The sun had risen, turning the river gold. Crows cawed, parrots shrieked, insects hummed in the warming air. The fat toad hopped over the deck to shoot out his sticky tongue. She sat up, feeling adrift, as if their houseboat had been cut from its chains and was floating towards a vast and unknown sea.

Who would take her in now? Her grandmother had been all the family she'd known, their shack on the Lally her only home. And why had Dima given her the tin elephant, yesterday, of all days? It was almost as if... But surely, if Dima had suspected she was in danger, she would have warned Minou?

Her head ached terribly, her eyes were swollen. She recalled her grandmother saying, *Father Jacob is a good man. You can trust him if anything should happen.* That was it – she'd go to Father Jacob. He'd asked her to do chores for his housekeeper, hadn't he? And he might help with Dima's funeral. The priest always treated her grandmother with respect, bowing if he met her on the street, and sending a bottle of rum and a pineapple each year for her birthday. Besides, no one else in Moonlally had the means to lend her the money – Nala owned less than she did, and Master Karu had his family and the homeless children of Blacktown to feed.

Later that morning, Minou pushed open the wrought-iron gate of Father Jacob's large yellow villa. She hesitated on the tiled path before the imposing mahogany door. It was held ajar with a brass doorstop, so anyone might enter – but the front entrance looked too grand for her. She stepped off the path and walked round to the back of the house.

The clatter of dishes and an aroma of frying onions drifted from behind a screen door. This must be the kitchen. She knocked firmly, but the cook let fly a string of curses and refused to call Father Jacob or Pinto, his housekeeper. Not knowing what else to do, Minou sat on the kitchen step, watching as the milk lady, the vegetable wallah and finally the knife sharpener came to conduct their business.

At last, the door flew open and Mrs Pinto appeared in a white sari, a look of disgust pursing her round face.

'Eh – be off with you! Don't come begging around here.'

Minou stumbled to her feet. 'I wasn't begging, ma'am. I'm here to see Father Jacob.'

'Nonsense, what on earth for?'

Minou swallowed, trying to find words to tell this stranger about Dima. She couldn't, not yet. 'Um…

yesterday – at church – Father said I was to come and help you with the chores? Polishing the floor and all that.'

Mrs Pinto was having none of it. 'A ragamuffin like you on my rosewood floors!' she cried, horrified. 'Father has strange ideas, but really.'

Minou blinked. The housekeeper's sari was starched a blinding white. Was it only yesterday she'd been caught by Father Jacob stealing two custard tarts? Yesterday Dima had been alive. And if Minou hadn't left her alone all day, she might be here now. Tears stung her eyes and blurred the housekeeper's round white shape.

Pinto frowned. 'Stop crying. Let me take a proper look at you.'

Minou sniffed, wiping her face with her tunic and drew herself straight.

'Well…' Pinto murmured. She pursed her lips, taking Minou's chin in her small plump fingers and turned her face one way and another. 'Perhaps Cook could do with some help. Come inside, but take off those filthy sandals.'

Barefoot, Minou followed Pinto across the marble-tiled kitchen, past the astonished cook and through a wide hallway. Here a staircase curved elegantly upwards, made from the same gleaming wood as the floor. The air was heavy with polish. Pinto halted suddenly, Minou colliding with her wide, sari-clad behind.

'Where do you think you're going? Stay in the kitchen!'

'Pinto!' The stairs creaked and Minou looked up to see Father Jacob. 'Miss Mignon is here at my invitation. We will take tea in the parlour, please.'

Father Jacob showed her to a large, cool room. Sunlight filtered through drawn white curtains; the heavy furniture was shrouded by cotton covers. The old priest lowered himself slowly on to the ghostly outline of an armchair. Minou stood, silently blinking back her tears.

'So, Mignon – you remembered to come and help Pinto, as we discussed. But where is your grandmother?'

She swallowed. Her skull ached; the stuffy room closing in upon her. *Gone.* Her Dima was gone, for ever. She didn't want to say the words aloud and make them real. '*Dima,*' she whispered, her throat tight in the airless room. She looked down at her brown toes, splayed on Father Jacob's silk rug.

'What's the matter, child?' Father Jacob's voice creaked with concern. 'Is Miss Rosa unwell?'

Minou shook her head and gulped. 'Dima's – gone, Father,' she told the priest with a sob. 'Yesterday, after church, I went to Blacktown. When I returned, she was dead. Her gun was on the floor – I think… someone killed her!'

'*Killed her?*' Father Jacob's tanned face drained to grey as he started from his chair. 'You mean… she was murdered? Are you sure?'

'Yes, Father. I'm sorry to trouble you – but I don't have a pagoda to pay for her funeral. Would you be so kind as to lend me the money? I can work here until I've paid you back…'

The old priest bowed his head, hands folded, his lips moving in silent prayer. Opening his eyes, he gave Minou a weary smile. 'Please, do not concern yourself, child. I will take care of the funeral expenses. Miss Rosa was a fine lady. But I'm afraid the police will have to be informed. They will need to see the body.'

Minou clutched dizzily at an armchair and murmured her thanks. *Body*. The word rang in her ears, heavy as lead.

'Your grandmother and I spoke of this, Mignon,' Father Jacob continued. 'In the event of her death, we agreed you were to be sent to the Home for Orphan Girls.'

'The Home for Orphan Girls?' Minou cried. 'By the Lady – why?' Dima would never have agreed to shut her away in a home. She'd heard they shaved off your hair and made you work from daybreak to midnight.

'Mignon, I see no other way.' Father Jacob leaned forward. 'Since your parents are gone—'

Minou's hand flew to the tin elephant. Surely Dima had given her the amulet for a reason? 'But Father Jacob—' she tugged it from under her tunic 'my mother left me this – it's all I have of her. Dima gave it to me the day she was killed. Someone might recognise it?'

Father Jacob held up his hand. 'I am certain your poor mother is dead, Mignon. I have never talked of the day I discovered you, have I, child?'

Minou shook her head. She knew the story from Dima, but Father Jacob had never spoken to her himself. The old priest leaned back in the armchair and closed his eyes. He was so still that, for a moment, Minou was frightened.

'You know I found you in a rowing boat, washed up on the banks of the Lally?'

'Yes, Father.'

'I was at the river searching for Tomas, my young curate. He'd been called out to baptise a baby.' The old priest shook his head. 'Alas, that night the great storm came. The waters rose and poor Tomas never returned. I found his boat wrecked on the bank and you – a helpless infant – bawling inside. Fit to wake the dead!' He smiled at her.

'What happened to him – to Tomas?'

Father Jacob rubbed his eyes. 'Tomas's body was dragged from the river a week later, child.'

'I'm sorry to hear that, Father. But I don't understand. What does that have to do with my mother?'

'Tomas was asked to baptise you. An urgent request on a stormy night. Mignon, I fear your mother was either dead or dying when Tomas reached her. I can think of no other reason he would bring you back in the boat with him.'

'And so... you gave me to Dima?'

'I knew Miss Rosa as a woman of impeccable character, may she rest in peace. I asked her to take you in as a favour. As she was already of considerable age, we agreed, if anything were to happen to her, you would be sent to the Home for Orphan Girls.'

'But, Father!' Minou broke in, alarmed. 'I'll hate it.'

Father Jacob sighed. 'It will do you good, Mignon. You're a clever girl, but without discipline, cleverness leads only to trouble. You will be taught to clean, cook and sew. One day, you'll have to make your own living and—'

The door flew open, interrupting him. The cook staggered in with a silver tray, laden with a teapot, cups, sandwiches and a fruitcake. He banged it down on the table with a resentful clatter and backed out of the room. Pinto, who'd been hovering by the door, bustled in. 'Don't trouble yourself, Father! I'll pour.'

'Ah, Pinto!' Father Jacob eased himself up from the armchair. 'I am sorry to say Mignon's grandmother died last night. The poor child is very upset. I think it's best she stays here tonight. Make up a bed in the servants' quarters.'

'Certainly, Father.' Pinto gave Minou a quick smile, her eyes glinting. 'I'll take good care of the little one.'

'Now, Mignon,' the old man cleared his throat. 'Please join me for tea.'

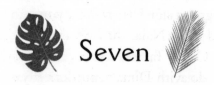

Seven

Minou climbed on to the undertaker's cart, taking her seat beside Pinto. Dima's funeral was to take place at Blacktown Cemetery that evening. Her coffin was strapped behind them. The housekeeper chattered on as they trundled through Whitetown and towards the river, but Minou was silent, staring at the shadows that stretched long and black across the Lally.

She felt as if she were being tugged along by the current with no way home. She hadn't eaten and had slept little on the floor of Pinto's room. There had been comings and goings – a policeman, who'd spent minutes questioning her, and an hour drinking tea with Pinto in the kitchen, while Father Jacob spoke to the Blacktown priest about arrangements for Dima's funeral.

Pinto had shooed her out to the villa gardens, where Minou wandered, until she spotted a cluster of green orchids by the pond. They grew everywhere, once you knew where to look. A bunch of the flowers, tied with grass, sat safely in her tunic pocket. If Dima had been a Green Orchid, the rebels would come to her funeral. Minou planned to place the flowers on Dima's tomb as a sign – a sign she was ready to join them. She remembered what Nala, the holy man, had said. *Ask your Dima.* Could Tal and Little's disappearance have anything to do with Dima's murder? If Jay was with the rebels today, she would ask him.

As they passed the riverbend, she turned to catch a glimpse of her old home. There were the Elephant Gates and the familiar wide curve of water, golden in the late afternoon sun. But where was Dima's shack? She stood, throwing back her veil.

'Mrs Pinto – Dima's houseboat. It's gone!'

Pinto sniffed. 'Of course it's gone. The police set fire to it. They should have got rid of that eyesore years ago.'

'Fire! They burned it down?' Minou's hand flew to her mouth. Tears stung her eyes at the thought of Dima's few possessions: her pipe, pots and pans, a few saris and the old flintlock pistol.

Only a fool stops to admire a tiger's nest, Dima would say, whenever Minou complained about their ramshackle home. Meaning that the person you were was more important than how grand your house was. But now the tiger's nest was gone – as if it had never existed.

She swallowed. 'What did that policeman say? The one you were talking to in the kitchen. Do they know who killed Dima?'

The housekeeper tutted. 'Robbery gone wrong. Blacktown's full of scoundrels these days.'

'But Dima had nothing to steal!'

Pinto was fanning herself with the *Moonlally Courier*. A picture of the *Napoleon* took up half of the front page, the headline read:

**GENERAL SURVIVES REBELS' ATTEMPT
ON THE NAPOLEON!**

The housekeeper snorted. 'You never can tell. These people live like paupers and hide gold under the floorboards! Sit down and lower your veil. This is a funeral, you know.'

Minou couldn't speak. Anger reared within her. How dare Pinto talk about Dima in that way? She was sure the police had blamed the murder on a robbery because they didn't care who'd killed her grandmother. She slumped into her seat, a hand on the tin elephant at her throat. To them, Dima was a poor old woman in a tumbledown shack. It didn't matter that she'd taken Minou in – or that her grandmother was afraid of nothing – not crocodiles, not tigers, not even the police.

'You look more respectable after a bath!' Pinto pinched Minou's cheek. 'What's this little trinket?' Her plump hand reached for the tin elephant.

'Nothing – only an amulet my mother left me.' Minou pulled it from Pinto's grasp and tucked it under her tunic. The tin elephant was all that was left of her life with Dima. She knew she should be grateful to

Pinto, who had lent her a black tunic and veil for the funeral, along with a fistful of glass bangles, but she felt an intense dislike for the woman. The tunic clung to her back in the humid air, her veil itched and the bangles' glassy chink annoyed her.

She turned towards the rushing green water as the cart rumbled over the bridge. When would she see the Lally again? Pinto had said they were to take the train directly after Dima's funeral. So much for Father Jacob's help – he'd bundled her off like a bag of unwanted old clothes, Minou thought bitterly. She'd have done better to hoist the houseboat's anchor, set sail and bury Dima at sea.

As they halted by the cemetery gates, the size of the gathered crowd surprised her. Minou had never been to a funeral before, and as few visitors came to their shack, she hadn't expected many mourners. Men in black topis, black-veiled women and children – the cemetery was thronged with people. Though it wasn't yet dark, every tomb blazed with candles in blackened glass jars.

'Blacktowners,' Pinto sniffed as they clambered from the cart. 'How they love a funeral! Might as well say "party", the way they'll turn up for free food and rum.'

The crowd parted to make way. Six young men stepped forward to lift Dima's coffin and bear it to the family tomb, Minou and Pinto following close behind.

Father Jacob had been generous. Inside the cemetery gates, decked with flowers, long tables covered in lace cloths were piled with fruit and pastries. Bottles of palm toddy and rice wine were lined up, ready for the mourners. Minou glanced at the pink dome of Blacktown Church. Dima had brought her here when she was little. She remembered the Blacktown ladies twittering around her tall, yellow-clad grandmother, like jungle birds around a prowling tiger. Dima preferred to pray at her home altar, where she lit a stick of jasmine incense and sang a hymn to the Dark Lady every morning. The Dark Lady might be a goddess from Moonlally's past, but she was still revered by Dima. Though even the Lady had not helped when Dima really needed her.

Over the clamour of voices, she was greeted by a thin young man whose eyes were lined with kohl, an accordion slung about his neck. Minou realised he was the Blacktown poet, Farisht, known for his funeral songs. He bowed to her and struck up a song in Dima's honour:

> *'Oh, Rosa, oh, Rosita!*
> *How strong you were, how kind.*
> *You left your husband – never mind.*
> *He was a drunk, they say and a cheater...*
>
> *Oh – beautiful, strong Rosita!*
> *You lived your life upon the water!*
> *Not a penny to your name.*
> *You cared nothing for honour or shame!*
> *You took an orphan for a granddaughter!*
>
> *Oh – beautiful, strong Rosita!'*

Funeral songs were a Blacktown tradition. They were sung for the dead, and also for those unlucky folk who had an enemy with five silver pagodas to spare – for that was Farisht's fee. Unlike songs for the dead, songs for the living were insulting and catchy – Minou often heard the Ragged School boys singing them.

She glanced about curiously as the funeral procession came to Dima's family tomb. The purple sky had deepened, and everywhere tiny candles glimmered into flame. The tombs of Blacktown Cemetery were small houses of stone, with flat roofs and heavy wooden doors. Blacktowners liked to be with their families in death, as in life.

Now, in the falling darkness, after her farewell to Dima, she could give Pinto the slip and join the Green Orchids. But if the rebels were here, they gave no sign.

The Blacktown priest mumbled words of prayer. Minou knelt, glad of the veil that hid her tears as her grandmother's body was carried inside the tomb. Pinto handed her a yellow lily. As she stooped to place it at the entrance, she let the bunch of green orchids drop alongside.

'These are for you, Dima,' she whispered. 'I'll never forget— *Ow!*' Pinto had grabbed her wrist and dug in her nails. 'Child! What are those?'

'The green flowers?' Minou asked innocently. 'I found them by the pond. I thought they were pretty…'

The priest gave Minou a horrified look and began to race through his prayers at top speed. Duties completed, he gathered up his robes and hurried off.

Pinto gripped her arm. 'Come now!' she scolded. 'We must leave – or we'll miss your train. These Blacktowners will keep up their gossiping and drinking half the night.'

'Stop! Let go of me!' Minou pulled free.

For the atmosphere had changed. Most of the guests had drifted away, but around Dima's tomb, a jostle of children remained – she recognised some as pupils of the Ragged School. A drum beat steadily under the lilt of Dima's song – the rhythm speeding faster, urged on by the clapping of the young men who'd carried Dima's coffin. They were tying black scarves over their faces.

Pinto gave a horrified yelp. 'I'll deal with you later!' she snapped, hitching up her tunic. 'I must notify the authorities. This is an unlawful gathering!'

Minou threw her veil back with delight now the housekeeper was gone. As the music surged louder, she strained to hear the words of the song, her mouth falling open in shock as they became clear.

> 'Beloved General!
> Oh, what a criminal!
> Your concern for the people
> Is minimal.
> You are a murderer.
> You killed our dear sister,
> Our rightful queen, did you
> Think we wouldn't miss her?
> You hunt our children's smiles

To feed your crocodiles.
You grind up their bones
To make the palace stones!
We pelted you with bombs
In your own kingdom.
You were indestructible
But now your end has come!

The funeral song was for the General! How wonderful to hear those words sung openly – she'd never known such defiance! The Green Orchids had turned out for Dima's funeral all right. But surely every one of them would be arrested? Minou felt the night breeze chill her skin and her heart leap with fear and excitement. As the tune rolled and bounced between the graves, she joined the singing voices.

Eight

Minou watched as the crowd thinned and candles were snuffed out one by one in a veil of grey smoke. The day's heat had faded and she shivered, feeling alarm seep into the air. Children huddled around her; their whispers as soft as the breeze blowing between the graves.

The masked young rebels of the Green Orchids were building a lean-to tent against the walls of the tomb. Silent as shadows, they lashed bamboo poles together and drove them deep into the earth. A bolt of black cloth billowed over the top. A clink of glass sounded beside her and a cup of palm wine was placed in her hands. She tried to sip the liquor, its touch burning her lips, but the cup was pulled from her mouth.

'Don't drink it, pour it out,' a familiar voice told her. 'At the feet of the Lady.'

A black clay icon of the Dark Lady – like the one on Dima's altar – stood at the entrance to her tomb. Minou poured the wine on the ground.

'Jay – you came. Thank the Lady!' she whispered, looking up with relief.

'Of course! I had to pay my respects to your grandmother.' Jay nodded towards the makeshift tent. 'So, this is your first meeting of the Green Orchids. I'm glad you've joined us.' He pointed to Minou's flowers at the entrance.

'Why is it in that tent?'

'I'll show you. Follow me!' He ducked inside, but Minou's way was blocked by a small boy. '*We have no hands, no face, no voice…*' he recited.

'Sparrow!' Jay's voice hissed. 'Say after me: *Like the Lady, we thrive in darkness.*'

Minou repeated his words and the boy waved her inside.

'*We have no hands, no face and no voice.*
Like the Lady we thrive in darkness.'

She said the words to herself. So the rebels, like Dima, followed the Dark Lady – goddess of Moonlally's queendom. She squeezed into the crowded space after Jay.

'Down here!' He patted a space beside him.

'Listen, Jay. Father Jacob wants to send me to the Home for Orphan Girls—'

Jay shook his head. 'We can't have that. I'll ask Karu to speak to him. He'll help you stay in Moonlally. Don't worry, Sparrow.'

'But where will I live?'

'Come to our place – Ma won't mind.'

'Are you sure?' Minou frowned. 'She won't make

me sew, like your sisters? I'm no good at that sort of thing.'

Jay's smile flashed, but before he could answer, Farisht's clear tones rose over the hum of voices.

'Friends! We are gathered here to bid farewell to our friend and beloved comrade. May the Dark Lady be with Miss Rosa on her journey.'

'May the Lady be with her,' the crowd murmured.

Minou blinked and swallowed down the tight feeling in her throat. She'd always thought Dima had no family in Moonlally – and now it turned out that she did. How she wished she'd known about the rebels before her grandmother had been killed.

'Today we welcome Miss Rosa's granddaughter, our newest recruit. *We have no hands, no face, no voice,*' Farisht chanted.

'*Like the Lady, we thrive in darkness,*' the crowd answered, Minou with them.

'And now – I have news of the insurgency!'

A dazzling light flickered above them and an image of the General's moustachioed face projected on to the white wall of the tomb.

'Tyrant! Bully!' voices yelled.

'Friends!' the poet cried. 'Our time is near. The tyrant's ridiculous airship caught fire. Behold!'

Children gasped as the General's face slid away, replaced by a painting of the *Napoleon* on fire. Flames blazed from the airship's gondola and licked over the purple silk balloon.

'According to the palace, he's alive – but a blow of resistance has been struck.'

Voices swelled around them.

'Silence, please!' Farisht called. 'There's more. I have messages from a Green Orchid who flourishes within the tyrant's fortress – yes, friends! There is a rebel *inside* the General's palace.'

'Is that really true?' Minou whispered to Jay.

'If Farisht says so. The resistance is growing, Sparrow, and you're part of it. Listen.'

'Miss Ophelia, the General's daughter, is to be married to a baron from the Whitetown land of Lutetia. Moonlally will fall further under Lutetian rule,' Farisht went on.

Jay nudged her. 'That was her – the girl we saw in the carriage. She's the Commandant's niece.'

Minou thought of the face at the lace-curtained window. The girl hadn't looked old enough to be married. But perhaps anything was better than being the General's daughter – even marrying a baron from faraway Lutetia.

'Our source tells us—' Farisht began. Just then, a whistle shrilled and a bell clanged in the distance.

'Police! Split up and run, friends. *Like the Lady we thrive in darkness*,' Farisht ordered.

Jay sprang up to help the others lift the tent over their heads and roll up the black cloth. Around them, the graveyard was emptying, children scurrying away through the labyrinth of tombs and disappearing into the night.

'Sparrow, run! This is a police raid – can you find your way to our place?'

Minou nodded, with more confidence than she felt.

'I'll see you later!' Jay faded into the shadows.

Minou looked frantically around her. She could see the lights of police torches, sweeping over the cemetery. Pinto had alerted the authorities, as she'd threatened, and would return for Minou. She needed to hide, but where? She didn't know the cemetery as well as the others.

'Hey, kid!' a voice called down from the roof of the tomb. She looked up to see Farisht. 'You haven't got time to get out of here now – you'd best hide.'

'What about you?' she asked. 'Shouldn't you hide?'

Farisht peered down at her. 'Ah, it's Miss Rosa's foundling. I live here – this graveyard's my home. Where would I go?'

'I liked the song you wrote for Dima,' she told him.

'Your grandmother was a great lady. A funeral song was the least I could do.' Farisht cupped a hand to his ear. 'Barking. Do you hear that? Police dogs. You can hide inside the tomb – they'll only flash a light at the entrance.'

Minou slipped through the open door, her feet crunching over glass shards and crushed petals. She was relieved that under candle smoke and palm wine, the inside smelled only of damp stone. She felt her way along the walls, slippery with moss. Dima's coffin rested upon its plinth, but Minou wasn't afraid. If her grandmother's spirit was anywhere, it was in her song's melody, the warm candlelight and faint scent of tobacco. Nothing of Dima remained here now.

Voices echoed, dogs snarled and yanked at their chains, as the policemen made their way through the graveyard.

'You! What are you doing up there?' a policeman shouted.

'I'm writing a song,' Farisht answered. 'Would you like to hear it?' He cleared his throat and started to hum.

'Shut up, fool! We're here to break up a meeting of insurgents—'

'You're mistaken. There was an old lady's funeral in the graveyard today. I sang her song myself.'

The policeman's stick cracked sharply against the wall. Minou jumped.

'We won't get anything out of this lunatic. Search the graveyard!' he spluttered.

'Officer!' Farisht called. 'Have you found Miss Rosa's murderer – the lady whose funeral we held today?'

'Not worth investigating,' the policeman's voice echoed loudly. He was standing right at the entrance. Minou held her breath. 'A failed robbery – the old woman waved her pistol; it went off and killed her. The thieves set her shack on fire to cover their traces.'

Minou let out a faint squeak of surprise. The man was lying! The shack hadn't been set alight until the day *after* Dima's death. And Pinto had told her the police were responsible. She pressed her lips tight and waited, heart galloping like a runaway pony, until the barking and voices faded.

Finally, she heard Farisht cry, 'Those goons have gone. Out you come, kid!'

Minou tiptoed from the musty tomb, ducking to avoid a bat swooping overhead. She was wary of bats, after being bitten as a baby. But Dima had been fond of them, even leaving a bowl of syrup on deck in the evenings, for night visitors to feast upon.

Farisht called down. 'Don't mind the bats. They're trained messengers, you know.'

'Messengers! How?'

'I've taught them. Right now, they're flying off over Blacktown, with the General's funeral song clutched in their tiny claws. Come and watch if you like.'

Minou clambered up on to the roof. A bat landed beside Farisht. He poured a drop of palm-wine on to his finger, which it licked with a pink tongue. He held out a tiny rolled paper and the bat screeched, curling its claws around the message and wheeling into the black sky.

'Like carrier pigeons – except with bats! So that's how your songs spread through the city so quickly. But what if the police find out?'

Farisht shrugged. 'Without danger, how do we know we're alive, hmm? Now, what are we going to do with you?'

'I'll be fine,' Minou told him. 'A friend's expecting me in Blacktown. Do you know Jay – Master Karu's brother?'

'Jay's one of us. He'll look after you.' The poet raised a hand in farewell. 'May the Dark Lady be with you. I have a feeling we'll meet again, in this world or the next!'

Farisht was kind, if a little eccentric, Minou decided, as she scrambled down from the roof. A few sputtering candles still glowed in the graveyard as she darted between tombs to reach the cemetery gates. Checking they were unguarded, she slipped through. The street was empty, the police long gone. She tore off her veil, making Pinto's glass bangles jingle, and breathed in the cool night air. A faint breeze fluttered at her tunic as she worked out the way to Master Karu's house.

Suddenly, muffled footsteps thudded behind her and a muscled arm closed round her like a trap. A damp cloth with a choking, chemical stench smothered her face. She bit and kicked, struggling to free herself, but the stranger's iron grip grew tighter and she was swallowed up in darkness.

Queen Amani, Warrior

Strife entered the south when invaders galloped
over the mountains, men with curved swords and
tall turbans. They'd heard of a beast, larger than a
brace of bears, armoured in tough hide and fearless.
When they saw warrior Queen Amani upon her
chief elephant, Rajah, towering over their horses,
and behind her a line of mounted soldiers, they
turned tail and fled.

From *A True History of the Queens of Moonlally*

II

In the Palace

Nine

Deep in her dream, Minou returned to her grandmother's funeral. She was hiding from the police in Dima's family tomb; the General's funeral song echoing around the graveyard. She stepped out into the eerie darkness, but the Green Orchids had disappeared. She was alone.

'Jay? Farisht! Where is everyone?' she cried out, floundering.

'Well, you can certainly sleep, young lady,' a voice replied sharply. 'I thought you'd never wake up!'

Minou forced her eyelids open, blinking as the dream mist lifted. Rubbing her eyes, she stared in confusion at the stranger frowning down at her. The woman looked like a Blacktowner but was dressed in Whitetown style, her white lace dress buttoned high in the neck. She snapped open a carved ivory fan to brandish at Minou, her wire-rimmed spectacles flashing as she peered at Minou's face.

'What a likeness! Sit up, so I can see you properly, child.'

Minou tried to obey, but her aching head rolled back on the pillow. She stared at the room's domed ceiling, painted indigo blue and glinting with gold stars. The woman reached to pull a cord above the bed. Bright light spilled from a ceiling lantern, making Minou screw her eyes shut. She'd never seen electric light indoors.

'Where am I?' she mumbled. Her head throbbed painfully. She tried to recall the previous evening at the cemetery. There had been a police raid and – she remembered now – as she stepped outside, someone had pressed a damp cloth with a medicinal smell over her face. After that, nothing.

With effort, she hauled herself upright and gaped at her surroundings. The bed was an ornate four-poster of shiny dark wood, a rose-pink marble floor stretched endlessly and the tall windows stood shuttered. A carved wooden almirah beside the bed was big enough to climb into, and the copper basin gleamed like a new coin. Had Pinto kidnapped her and dragged her to the Home for Orphan Girls after all? But if so, the place was much grander than she'd expected. Dima's shack would fit inside this room ten times over.

'Is this the Home for Orphan Girls?' she asked.

'Home for Orphan Girls! Dear me, no.' The woman handed her a silver tumbler of water which she gulped thirstily. 'This, child, is the General's palace. And I am your governess. You may call me Mamzelle.'

Minou nearly choked. 'The *palace*? By the Lady and her thundering elephants!'

The woman wagged a finger sternly. 'You have been chosen for the favoured position of Shadow to the General's daughter. Please mind your language accordingly.'

'Shadow?' Minou was bewildered. 'Look, you've got it wrong. I wasn't chosen, any more than a chicken gets chosen from market. Someone grabbed me!'

'There has been no mistake,' the woman told her. 'Forget your old life. Your fortunes are transformed. Now, you will live in luxury!' She swept her arm to gesture at the vast bedchamber.

'But – I don't want to live here!' Minou hopped off the bed, stumbling on legs that felt stuffed with cotton. She staggered to the door and rattled the silver doorknob. It was locked. 'Let me go, or I'll scream for help – palace or no palace!'

Mamzelle gave a tight smile. 'Screaming would be ill-mannered and pointless. There's no one to hear you but the mechanical guards.'

'Mechanical what? But you don't understand – I'm not staying here!'

'Would you prefer the Home for Orphan Girls? I'm sure we can find some poor girl to trade places.'

'My friends are waiting for me in Blacktown! They'll be worried if I don't turn up.'

'Is that so? Tell me the address and I shall have a message sent to them.' The governess took the glass from her.

A cold fear seized Minou. Jay was a rebel – she couldn't send a message to his house. Tal and Little were missing, and now here she was, under lock and key. She wouldn't put Jay and his family in danger too.

She shook her head mutinously.

The hard lines of the governess's face softened. 'Child. You arrived late last night and must be famished, I'm sure.' She picked a porcelain cup from a table by the bed and held it out to Minou. 'Drink this milk and rest. I'll bring your breakfast later.'

Minou swayed on her legs. She couldn't remember when she'd last eaten – she'd hardly taken a bite at Father Jacob's. She drank the sweetened milk and was at once overcome with drowsiness. Mamzelle helped her clamber back into bed, where she sank into a dreamless sleep.

Hours later, she woke with a dull ache boring at her skull. She'd fallen asleep almost instantly. Had the milk been drugged – like the cloth pressed over her face outside the cemetery? Well, she wouldn't be caught out a third time. From now on, she'd refuse every crumb of food.

Surely Mamzelle would have to let her out before she starved?

And if she didn't? No matter how loudly she yelled, no one would hear. The palace was a secret city within the city, hidden behind high walls. Now Dima was dead, who'd care that she'd disappeared? Father Jacob would think she was at the home – and Pinto wouldn't admit she'd let Minou slip through her fingers. Jay would search for her but he'd never find her, locked up in this marble mausoleum.

She darted across the room, twisted the doorknob and rattled the door again. *Locked.* Dragging a chair over to the window, she leaped up to wrench the shutters open. The windows were not glass but stone, carved with a trellis pattern of flowers. This allowed air and light to enter the room but made it impossible to climb out. By the Lady! What did the General want with *her*? What was a Shadow, anyway? Some sort of maid, she guessed.

A dove cooed by the window, fluffing its white feathers. Minou whistled back, resting her face against the cool stone. Outside the window, she glimpsed a terrace with greenery and heard the sound of running water. As she listened, the palace clocks began to ring out the hour, one after another, like great brass gongs.

How would she ever escape?

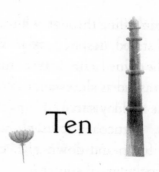

Ten

'**B**reakfast!' Mamzelle trilled as the chamber door flew open. The governess carried a silver tray, piled with more food than Minou had ever seen. Saffron rice pudding with honey, soft cardamom-scented bread rolls, fruits carved like jewels and a silver jug of steaming coffee.

Minou grimaced. Her head throbbed furiously from the drugged milk and her stomach rumbled as she folded her arms. 'I'm not hungry.'

'Don't be foolish, child.'

'I won't eat a single crumb,' she grumbled through gritted teeth. 'Not after you poisoned my milk.'

'That was merely a sleeping draught. Surely you must be famished?'

Minou clamped her lips tightly together and shook her head.

Mamzelle sighed. 'Well. I don't expect missing breakfast this once will hurt. Time to get dressed, then.' She walked over to the almirah, flung the doors open and began rifling through white dress after white dress. Minou stared, despite herself. When she'd lived with Dima, she owned a single set of tunic and trousers, which were washed as she swam in the river and dried on deck in the midday sun.

'Bloomers, petticoats, corset...' Mamzelle gave Minou a swift up-and-down glance. 'Lace dress – you'll need stockings, of course.'

Minou slid off the bed and watched the governess pour a jug of steaming hot water into the copper basin.

'But first, a proper wash. I see Pinto gave you a good scrubbing, but you're not up to my standards yet. Under the fingernails and behind the ears.'

Minou was more puzzled than ever. '*Pinto?*' What did Father Jacob's housekeeper have to do with anything?

'You have Pinto to thank for your position as Shadow. Her husband is an officer of the General's police. She told him of your resemblance to Miss Ophelia.' The governess unwrapped a bar of pink soap and placed it by the basin

'Resemblance? I don't understand. By the Lady, what is a Shadow, anyway?'

'You know that Miss Ophelia will marry into one of Lutetia's noblest families. The marriage begins a new chapter in the history of Moonlally.'

Minou thought of the girl she'd seen in the carriage window. 'Why? What difference does it make who she marries?'

Mamzelle raised her eyebrows. 'Our ruling family will be connected with Lutetian nobility! The

General and Commandant do not dare expose Miss Ophelia to any danger from troublesome rebels. So her Shadow – that's you, dear – will take her place for public appearances.'

'You mean I'm a double – for the General's daughter?'

'Exactly so,' Mamzelle continued. 'Miss Ophelia visits Father Jacob for spiritual guidance, so Pinto knows her. What luck for you, child! Only think – you will dine on the finest food and possess the second-best wardrobe in Moonlally. Now, please wash and dress. When I return, we begin lessons in the schoolroom.' The door slammed shut. Mamzelle bustled away, the jangle of her keys fading to silence.

Minou bumped her head on the copper basin and groaned. Whatever the likeness between herself and Ophelia, she knew the housekeeper had betrayed her because she was alone in the world. No one would notice she was missing – or care if she lived or died. She twisted the towel in her hands. How she'd love to wring that interfering Pinto's neck!

She sighed and splashed her face clean. There was no point feeling sorry for herself. At Dima's funeral, Farisht had said there was a Green Orchid inside the palace. She'd try to contact them, whoever they were, and send out a message. For now, she would pretend to go along with Mamzelle's plans. She wasn't going to find the rebel locked up in her marble chamber.

Puzzled, she stared at the pile of frilly clothes Mamzelle had laid out on the bed. Which went underneath and which on top? She decided to leave off the corset, which looked uncomfortable, pulling on a white dress and stockings and stuffing her feet into a pair of heavy boots. She hid the tin elephant under the collar of her dress, which fastened from neck to hem with fiddly ivory buttons. No wonder Whitetown ladies always looked cross, they must spend half the day dressing and undressing. Mamzelle entered as she was braiding her tangled hair.

'*Fiddlesticks!*' The governess took a step backwards, her hands flying up in horror. 'Your stockings are wrinkled. No corset or petticoat, and as for your *coiffure*, dear me…' She insisted on brushing Minou's hair herself, tugging painfully at the knots. Once she was satisfied, she led her out of the bedroom to a walled terrace.

'Hurry now, we must not be tardy. I have much to teach you.'

Minou took a deep breath of balmy air. Living on the flowing river, she was used to open skies. Walls and ceilings, however beautifully decorated, made her head hurt. She scanned the terrace for likely escape routes, but it was enclosed by a high wall of carved stone, exactly like the windows in her room. She looked around for something she might use to climb the wall but saw only orange trees in pots and a curious fountain. Water flowed from a brass bowl into a channel that ran along the blue-tiled floor.

The governess was watching her. 'That is one of our famous water clocks, Mignon. You'll see them everywhere in the palace. When the bowl fills, it tilts down, water spills out and a brass gong sounds to mark the hour.'

Minou skated her fingers along the water's cool surface. The jasmine scent made her chest tighten, reminding her of the incense Dima lit. How different the palace was from their shack on the river – here even the water was perfumed.

'Come along,' the governess called as she unlocked a barred iron gate at the far end of the terrace. 'Don't mind the mechanical. He won't hurt us.'

Minou gaped as an armoured guard glided forward and the gate swung slowly open. He was huge, his shiny metal breastplate looming above them. An axe with a sharply glinting blade was slung over his giant shoulder, and the eye sockets in his helmet were empty black hollows. So that was how the guards outside the palace stood the heat all day! They were mechanicals, with no more feeling than a machine. She shook her head in disbelief as she followed Mamzelle.

The General's palace was a most peculiar place.

Eleven

Minou glanced back warily at the sinister mechanical guard, as she followed the clipped sound of Mamzelle's boots across the courtyard. The deserted space was surrounded by once grand buildings, overgrown with moss and creepers, their white walls as yellow as the tobacco stains on Dima's fingers. Each dilapidated door they passed was locked and every window barred. The whole place had a sad, neglected air.

'Why is it so quiet, Mamzelle? Where is everyone?'

'This part of the palace is not much in use,' Mamzelle told her. 'We have the run of the place.'

'But where does the General live? What about his wife and daughter – and all their servants?' More importantly, where was the rebel Farisht had spoken of?

'Why, in the fortress. It's a proper castle, towers, battlements, crenellations – quite a picture. Every stone was shipped from Lutetia. The General had it built on the site of the Temple of the Dark Lady. I

advise you not to venture into that part of the palace –
if they catch you, you'll be thrown to the crocodiles.
Ha!' The governess gave a mirthless laugh.

'*Crocodiles?*' Surely Mamzelle was joking. But
before she could ask more, the governess bustled her
up a flight of stairs to a terrace like her own, complete
with water clock.

From the terrace, Mamzelle threw open panelled
doors to the high-ceilinged schoolroom. Minou gazed
about her in wonder at the bookshelves, framed maps
and botanical prints lining the walls. She was used to
lessons under the mango tree in Master Karu's dusty
courtyard. The sharp scents of herbs, ink and paper
prickled her nose. A marble countertop was laden
with dried plants, glass bottles and jars. She tried
to decipher the labels, written in a curly script and
accompanied by strange symbols: an eye, a heart and
a grinning skull.

'Be sure you don't touch my herbs and tinctures,
Mignon, they are for medicinal use. Come and look at
the orrery we use to study astronomy. Have you ever
seen anything so wonderful?'

Minou gasped in astonishment at the schoolroom's
centrepiece. A glittering brass model of the sun was
suspended from the ceiling, beside it hung a metal
globe of the earth, enamelled in blue and green and
spinning in orbit with the other planets. There was
even a silver moon.

Mamzelle smiled. 'Isn't it a marvel? Designed by
the palace clockmaker.'

'Is that the clockmaker who built the General's elephant?'

Mamzelle's smile vanished. She shot Minou a stern look. 'You must learn not to ask questions, Mignon. Curiosity is out of place in a lady.'

In which case, Minou wondered, why bother with lessons or a schoolroom at all?

Mamzelle directed her to a wooden table and chair and placed a sheet of sums before her. The morning passed slowly, with tests in reading, writing, arithmetic and more. Minou did well, for Master Karu was an excellent teacher, but the geography and history she'd learned were very different to Mamzelle's requirements and she had never studied natural philosophy or astronomy.

As the morning dragged on, Minou tugged out the hairpins digging into her scalp and lined them up on the desk before her. The lace of her dress itched terribly, its high collar strangled her neck and her heavy boots were lead weights on each foot. How she longed for her old tunic and trousers – she'd be able to concentrate so much better.

'Do not fidget, child! Must I dose you with flea powder?'

'Sorry, Mamzelle – these clothes are different to what I'm used to.'

Lunchtime could not have come too soon. Mamzelle brought in bowls of thin brown soup and a plate of rolls. 'Bone broth! A light and nutritious luncheon is best for scholars – to feed one's mind!'

Minou was disappointed at the frugal lunch, compared with the delicious breakfast she'd turned down. But seeing Mamzelle sharing it with her, she knew it was at least safe to eat, without fear of being drugged.

After lunch, the governess opened an enormous book, bound in faded red leather. 'Time to practise your sketching, Mignon, a skill ladies ought to have. This tome is precious, handle it carefully. It is a rare first edition of Gaston d'Aragord's *Botanica of Southern Indica*. You may copy the flowers in watercolour, while I prepare remedies next door. I have an interest in herbal medicine – all the servants come to me for their little illnesses,' she explained.

Mamzelle swept out to a room across the passage and left her to it. Minou enjoyed drawing, though she'd never had more than a slate and broken chalk at Master Karu's school. The pencils and tin of watercolours Mamzelle had left filled her with delight, and she experimented with mixing new shades, before turning to the thick, crinkled pages of the old book with its musty smell and paintings of flowers and plants.

D'Aragord's *Botanica* was filled with medical cures – most for mystifying illnesses such as dropsy and gout. Minou found an instruction for a sleeping potion and wondered if it might be the one Mamzelle had used in her milk. She decided to memorise it, just in case. Along with flowers, there were paintings of insects, birds and even the odd snake. She painted a bunch of mallow blooms to show Mamzelle, and copied a tiny sparrow in sepia and chestnut, pocketing the paper for herself.

Through the doorway, she saw Mamzelle stirring a glass container of yellow liquid over a low flame, her spectacled face hidden behind a cloud of smoke. Minou realised this was the perfect time to explore. Silently, she unlaced her boots and slipped them off under the table. She tiptoed out of the room and along the passage. If she was caught, she'd say she was looking for the bathroom.

A staircase led to the first floor. Upstairs, she discovered a bedchamber – this must be where Mamzelle slept. The door opened into a pretty room, half the size of her own, with a four-poster bed hung in white muslin, a ceiling painted with birds and a window seat upholstered in green velvet. Under the lid of the window seat were books in worn leather bindings and a black lacquer music box. Minou opened it and a tinny waltz began to play, a pair of tiny figures in evening dress spinning in circles. They were detailed down to their glass eyes and a beaded choker around the woman's neck. Watching them gave her the strangest feeling, as if they were real people, imprisoned by some enchantment.

'Mignon! *Mignon!* Where have you got to, child?' Mamzelle's voice echoed from below and Minou heard her heavy tread on the stairs. With a start, she thrust the music box in her pocket, ran to the washbasin and dabbed at her sleeve.

'What are you doing up here, Mignon?'

'Oh, Mamzelle – I spilled paint on my sleeve and was afraid you might be cross if you saw it. What a pretty room! Is this where you sleep?'

'Yes, this was the young queen's room. I would have given it to you, but it's close to the elephant stables and the animals make a terrible racket – not to mention the smell!' The governess wrinkled her nose and fanned her face.

'Elephants! How I'd love to see them...'

'If you're good, I will take you one evening. But you must remain in your quarters by day. It would not do for all and sundry to know of Miss Ophelia's Shadow. Luckily, servants won't come to the old palace. Only the mahouts who look after the elephants – and even they don't dare visit at night.'

'Why not?'

'They believe the old palace is haunted. Superstitious nonsense, of course.'

'*Haunted?*' Minou wanted to learn more, but remembering Mamzelle's warning about questions, she dried her hands and patted the black lacquer box, safe in her pocket.

The palace might be full of secrets, but she was determined to puzzle them out.

Twelve

Minou was not used to sleeping alone, and that night in the palace, she was plagued by nightmares. She was plunged back to the eve of Dima's death, the stench of rusted iron and gunpowder filling their shack. From the wall, the General's white-painted face glared at her, his black eyes as empty as the holes in the mechanical guard's helmet. A restless wind rocked the boat and the pots and pans hanging from hooks rattled.

She woke at a loud bang, heart racing. There'd been a rain shower, the blustering wind had blown her shutters open. She shivered and sat up, rubbing her eyes, the terror of her dream vividly alive. It was true – on the night she'd found Dima, the portrait of the General hadn't been turned away as it usually was. His face had stared down from the wall as she'd crouched, sobbing, over her grandmother's body. Whoever killed Dima had also turned the General's portrait face out. That policeman at Dima's funeral had lied about setting their shack on fire. Had the police covered for Dima's murderer?

Cool air blew into her chamber, bringing the fresh scent of rain. A movement by the window caught her eye. Her heart stuttered, but it was only her dress, hung over a chair, skirts fluttering in the breeze. Or was it? The fine hairs on her neck prickled with fear. The air felt electric, expectant – as if before a storm. Something stirred by the open shutter. As she stared in confusion, dense black smoke billowed into her room, moving through the latticed stone and over the moonlit floor. The wind rose and her shutters banged closed. Dumbstruck, she watched the darkness spiral from the floor, taking on a shape – hazy at first. The unmistakeable figure of a woman stood before her, face shadowed, eyes glowing with amber light.

Mamzelle had said the old palace was haunted – but this was no ghost! Minou knew, like Dima, she'd been visited by the spirit of the Dark Lady – goddess of Moonlally. Desperately, she tried to remember how to behave in the goddess's presence. Sliding off the bed, heart racing, she sank to kneel on the cold marble floor, clasping her hands in prayer and lowering her eyes.

'Dark Lady. Cloudborn, Rainmaker, Lightning striker, Tide-turner, Moon dazzler...' she murmured, struggling to recall all thirteen names of the goddess. Dima had sung a hymn to the Lady each morning at her altar. Minou wished she'd paid more attention.

'Storm summoner, Pearl giver?' Curious, she glanced up to meet the Lady's amber gaze. Pale light streamed from the shadowy figure's brow, flooding the dark room in silver radiance. Heat flushed Minou's face, blood pulsed in her ears, and the room around her tilted and spun.

When Minou awoke hours later, her room was awash in sunlight. Uncurling stiffly from the floor, she hugged herself, rubbing life into her cramped arms. It was morning. She'd fainted, most likely from lack of food. And the Dark Lady had vanished. Only the scent of rain told Minou she hadn't imagined the whole thing. She collapsed on to her bed and stared at the blue-domed ceiling, glimmering with stars.

Respect the Dark Lady, Dima had told her. The first time the Dark Lady appeared to her grandmother was the night of the great storm, the night Minou was saved from drowning. Ever since, Dima had believed fervently that the goddess protected her. Was it true?

Mamzelle had said that the General's new fortress was built on the Temple of the Dark Lady – little wonder her spirit roamed the palace at night. How foolish of the servants, to mistake the goddess for a ghost! Minou sighed, wishing she could talk about what she'd seen. Mamzelle would never believe her. If it hadn't been for Pinto, she'd be in Blacktown, with Jay and his sisters for company, not locked in this marble tomb. She smiled, thinking how thrilled Jay would have been with this adventure. He'd told her a Green Orchid must act like a cobra, slinking silently under the walls to deliver its deadly bite.

Minou sat up. Well, if Jay could be a cobra – so could she. She'd already slunk inside the palace walls! All she needed to do was find the other Green

Orchid – they'd work together. They could even rescue Tal and Little. Dima had been fearless – a rebel to the end. Perhaps the Dark Lady wanted her to take Dima's place – to act like the Green Orchid she was.

Minou jumped off the bed and shook out her stiff limbs to begin her kalari warm-up. She'd need to exercise every day and eat properly, to keep up her strength. She was a Green Orchid and she wouldn't forget it.

Later that morning, Mamzelle arrived with breakfast. To her surprise, she found Minou fully dressed, stockings and all, hair scraped into a tight bun. 'You certainly learn fast, Mignon! From today you may take the air on your terrace whenever you wish. I will leave your room unlocked. I have brought rice porridge for breakfast. I'll taste it, so you know it hasn't been tampered with.'

Mamzelle lifted a silver spoon to taste the porridge. Minou could not be sure she was telling the truth but ate the whole bowl anyway. On their way to the schoolroom, Minou watched carefully as the governess unlocked the iron gate and the guard wheeled forward. A single gate and a mechanical wouldn't stop a cobra exploring the palace. All she had to do was slink past them.

Lessons that day began with geography. Minou enjoyed spinning the blue and green globe, fingers flying over the surface, as she named the territories of Lutetia, Britannia and Hispania. She'd always been quick at learning – Master Karu had often remarked on it. This had not made her popular with the other pupils at the Ragged School. She tried her best not to scratch or fidget, preparing to be a silent cobra in the palace for the rebels – though her itchy lace dress would take getting used to.

'Today we will study Lutetia in depth, its ancient ruins, castles and churches,' Mamzelle announced.

'Ruins? I didn't know it was an ancient city, Mamzelle?' Minou tried to sound interested.

'It was founded by the Romans! But the ruins are surpassed by the wonders of the new city. The Iron Tower of Lutetia is the tallest building in the world – that's where the *Napoleon* docks.'

'The *Napoleon*? But, Mamzelle – wasn't the airship blown up?'

'Indeed not. Only a small fire in the engine room. The *Napoleon* is in excellent repair for your voyage.'

'Will we travel together, Mamzelle, to Lutetia?'

'I must sail with Miss Ophelia, who will journey by ocean steamer to her wedding. You will be accompanied by the Shadow General and Wife.'

Minou blinked. 'Oh. But the *real* General and his wife? Won't they go to their own daughter's wedding?'

'They remain in Moonlally. The General has not left the palace in years. Enough chatter. You must apply yourself, Mignon, we have so little time before the voyage. And why no corset?'

Minou shrugged. 'I left it off, Mamzelle – I've never worn one. How much time do we have – before the airship takes flight?'

The governess tutted. 'Days, mere days, and several tasks still to be completed. But you'll need the corset to wear Miss Ophelia's dresses. As her Shadow, you have a copy of every gown, lucky girl! While I remember, let us try them on. I fear alterations will be needed.'

Minou followed the governess up the staircase, befuddled by how quickly everything was happening. She was to be shipped to Lutetia on the *Napoleon* any day now. Which meant, she'd have to act fast to find the Green Orchid in the palace.

As she entered the bedchamber, she patted her pocket for the music box, planning to replace it, but she'd left it in her own room. Worse, on the window seat in front of them was her watercolour of a sparrow – she'd dropped it yesterday. Hastily, she snatched it up as Mamzelle marched over to fling open the almirah. Thank the Lady the governess was short-sighted.

'Mignon, look! Such elegance. All made from the finest silk – and the colours! Rose gold, lavender and sea blue. Scandalous to Moonlally eyes, but in Lutetia, bright colours are the custom. Try the embroidered blue day dress first. Lift your arms.'

Minou struggled into the dress, its hem trailing on the floor. 'It's much too long, Mamzelle.'

'Ten centimetres in length and five at the waist. Even with no corset!' the governess tutted through a mouthful of pins. 'Though you are like Miss Ophelia in the face, your build is inferior. Now the ballgown. Silk with red crystal beading. Miss Ophelia's gown is gold tussore embroidered with real rubies.'

Minou gazed at the elaborate gown. *Gold tussore with real rubies.* Where had she heard those words before? Of course – at Master Karu's! This was the dress she'd seen his mother and sisters embroidering. She touched the rich gold cloth and wondered how to send Jay a message. In her pocket was the small watercolour painting of a sparrow. If he saw it, perhaps he'd realise she was a prisoner in the palace?

'Hold still while I pin the hem. How trying! Everything will need to be altered,' Mamzelle muttered crossly. 'Where are my embroidery scissors?'

The governess turned away for an instant and Minou slid her painted sparrow into the pinned hem of the gown. She closed her eyes and sent up a swift prayer to the Dark Lady, that it might wing its way to Jay.

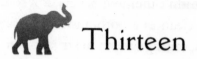

Thirteen

That evening, Minou slipped the black tunic she'd worn at Dima's funeral from under her mattress and pulled it over her white lace frock. As night fell, she crept along her terrace, heart bumping like a cart on a Blacktown road. She peered through the gate, eyeing the mechanical guard's battle-axe, glinting menacingly in the moonlight. The guard wasn't *real*, she reminded herself. All she had to do was run up, climb the gate and haul herself over the top.

Taking a few steps back, she caught sight of a figure, hurrying through the courtyard. A girl, dressed in white tunic and trousers. Was she a servant? But Mamzelle said the servants refused to come to this part of the palace at night, because they were afraid of the ghost – or rather, the Dark Lady. Minou took a swift run, leaped high to grab the crossbar and clung tight to the spikes as she pulled herself over the top of the gate. Easy!

But as she slid down the other side, the mechanical guard swivelled forward, axe raised. Minou dived to the floor, rolling free just as his weapon wheeled down to strike the gate. An ear-splitting metallic clang shattered the courtyard's calm. She winced and rubbed her neck. If she hadn't jumped, her head would have been hacked off, clean as a coconut from a tree. The guard rolled back, raising his axe to strike again.

Crouched on the ground, Minou blew out a long sigh. Had Mamzelle been woken by the clash of metal? She hoped not. She'd have to get past the guard again, somehow – but she'd worry about that later. She stood up and dusted herself off, ready to explore. Where had that servant girl disappeared to? A full moon had risen, bleaching the dilapidated buildings ivory. It was clear the courtyard around her was deserted.

Minou could hear the palace elephants, stirring their feet and trumpeting. Perhaps the girl was one of the mahouts? She decided to find the stables, following a strong smell of elephant dung. Keeping close to the walls, she darted along the shadows. She came to a wide brick building, with giant arched doorways and a row of domed roofs. The smell of dung was strongest here – these must be the stables. Minou tiptoed closer and peered into the darkness. Banana skins were scattered on the ground – the girl must have just fed the animals. A great grey head loomed above her. The elephant raised its trunk and snorted.

Minou gazed into its tiny, unblinking eyes. 'Hello!' she whispered. 'Aren't you beautiful? What a shame you're locked up in here.' Back in the time of the queendom, it must have been wonderful to see the elephants parade through the gates to splash in the Lally.

A flight of stairs led to the stable roof. She stole up the steps, skirting around the domes. In the centre was a raised parapet, like a platform or stage. Minou waited, listening for footsteps. All was silent, so she crept on to the parapet to look out over the palace. Dima had told her that the palace had been open to all on Sundays. There had been refreshments, and entertainment from musicians who made their stage on the stable roof, while the elephants swayed to the drumbeat.

From her new vantage point, she could see a set of iron gates which led to the inner palace and the General's fortress, on the site of the Dark Lady's Temple. Its vast walls were grey stone with narrow slits for windows, only faint bars of light stealing through. Four high towers, one at each corner, flew his gold-on-purple elephant flag at their pinnacles. Bats swooped around the towers, flitting into the blue-black night. The castle was surrounded by a wide silver moat, a bridge over it led to tall wooden doors, bounded with iron and flanked by armoured guards – mechanicals, she was sure. She'd sneaked past one already. But dare she enter the General's palace?

Minou heard a gate creak and squinted into the darkness. The servant girl floated through, making her way to the fortress. She watched her small figure crossing the bridge as a knobbly head surfaced from the gleaming moat, its yellow eyes bulging. She gulped.

Mamzelle hadn't joked about the crocodiles – those were certainly not mechanicals.

The girl's white shape vanished into the castle. Minou hurried down from the stable roof to set off after her, when she noticed a weathered green door swinging open. The servant girl had come from wherever this door led. She looked around her. The courtyard was empty. She slipped through and found herself in a narrow space, moonlight filtering from a high barred window. A scent of incense and candlewax lingered. She spotted a chain hanging from the ceiling and pulled it. Coloured lights bloomed in the darkness, revealing a figure on a platform, profile silhouetted by the soft light. It was an icon of the Dark Lady, draped in silver cloth, with two glowing rubies for eyes. This room was a makeshift temple.

Minou edged closer. She knew from Dima that the Temple of the Dark Lady once held a precious icon of the goddess, carved in ebony wood with ruby eyes and a black diamond set in her forehead – her magical third eye. This had to be the Lady from the original temple, but now an empty hollow marred her forehead. Her third eye, the priceless black diamond of Moonlally, was gone. Who was foolish enough to steal from a goddess?

Lowering her eyes, Minou folded her hands and whispered the names of the Lady she remembered: *Cloudborn, Rainmaker, Lightning striker, Tide-turner, Moon dazzler, Storm summoner, Pearl finder, Sorrow healer, Song weaver, Elephant tamer...* She touched the tin elephant, warm at her throat, wishing again she'd listened to Dima's prayers.

As her eyes grew accustomed to the light, she noticed a door at the far end of the room. Surely only a rebel would make a secret temple for the Dark Lady! Would she find the Green Orchid here? Heart thumping with excitement, Minou tiptoed to the door and pushed it open, stepping into a cavernous room lit by yellow gaslight.

She blinked. Dismantled bicycles, umbrellas and rubber tyres cluttered the floor, with boxes spilling screws, springs and bolts. Old mattresses were heaped in the centre. Around the walls, huge objects stood shrouded in pale covers. Minou's nose tickled and she almost sneezed. The room was a warehouse, but it wasn't only for storage – the scent of wood shavings was fresh in the air. This was a workshop.

'Hello! Is anyone here?' she called, her voice echoing in the vaulted space. No one answered, but a high squeak sounded above – a circling bat. She ducked, suppressing her scream as the gloom dissolved into hundreds of bats, roosting in the rafters of the old warehouse and flocking down at the sound of her voice. She flapped at them fearfully, backing into the corner and stumbling against one of the shrouded objects that lined the walls.

Curious, she tugged at the draped cover and gasped in delight. The General's elephant! Or a copy – for this elephant was smaller than the painting she'd seen at Master Karu's. Made from mahogany wood with polished brass fittings, it was small enough that she could reach to stroke the dome of its head. She looked at the other shapes, wondering what they might be.

'Arms wide, knees bent!' Minou spun round in surprise at the voice and spotted a metal platform lodged below the high ceiling. A long ladder led to where a black-clad figure stood, extending two wide – could those really be *wings*?

With a strange cry, the figure swooped off the platform into flight, gliding a short distance to land with a tumble and noisy crash on top of the mattresses.

Fourteen

'By the *Lady*!' Minou whispered, astonished. An elderly man clambered from the pile of mattresses, his ribbed black silk wings trailing behind. With his helmet and huge goggles, he appeared more giant insect than human. She hurried over to him. 'Are you all right?'

'No bones broken!' the man chortled, taking off his helmet and unfastening the harness. 'It's in the take-off angle, you know. But who are you? I mistook you for someone else.' He shrugged off the wings and peered at her in the half-light.

'I – my name's Mignon. But most people call me Sparrow.'

He frowned. 'Well, Sparrow,' he said. 'I don't know about you, but after that adventure, I could do with a cup of chai.'

Minou perched on an armchair, watching in fascination as her new acquaintance made chai over a small kerosene stove. He had no right hand, but the stump of his wrist was covered in a shiny metal cap with a pincer attachment. He shook tea leaves and sugar into a metal pan, deftly adding water from a pitcher and lighting the stove with a nearby candle.

'So! What brings you here?' he asked.

'I'm Shadow to Miss Ophelia. Though no one's supposed to know.' Minou told him of Dima's death and the events after her funeral, leaving out the part about the Green Orchids. She didn't know for certain that he was one of the rebels. 'Then I woke up in the palace, with Mamzelle leaning over me,' she concluded.

'That must have been a nasty shock. Careful – it's hot!' he remarked, handing her a clay cup of fragrant chai. Minou took a gulp of the steaming drink.

'Wait a minute – ow!' she cried, spilling her tea in excitement. 'I've just realised who you are!'

'Who am I?'

'You're Shri, the famous clockmaker! Inventor of Moonlally's Magnificent Elephant and other wonders. You made the orrery in the schoolroom. And clockwork toys for the young queen – jewelled hummingbirds and golden bees—' She stopped, worried that she'd been tactless in speaking of the past. 'I'm so sorry – about what the General did to your hand,' she added.

To her surprise, the man chuckled.

'So, you have heard of me.' He took a sip of tea. 'Alas, most of my inventions have been melted down. Once, I made battalions of mechanical beasts and aviaries of clockwork birds! But the General prefers different toys. Weapons, mostly. My mechanicals are all he has any use for.'

Minou flinched as a bat swooped down to rest on her battered armchair, folding its shiny black wings and hunching its small, furred head.

'Don't worry about the bats – they're harmless. In fact, they inspired my latest invention.'

'Those batwings?' she asked, eyeing the creature warily as it took flight, wheeling to the high windows. 'They're amazing – I can't believe I saw you fly!'

'That was gliding rather than flying, to be precise,' Shri corrected. 'Those batwings are escape gliders – to evacuate the airship *Napoleon* in case of emergencies.' He peered closer at Minou, as if seeing her for the first time. 'So, you're Miss Ophelia's Shadow? Well, that explains the likeness. But why are you wandering around the old palace, child – didn't that Mamzelle woman warn you about the ghost?'

'I'm not scared of ghosts. Anyway, she's not a ghost – she's the Dark Lady!'

Shri nodded. 'I'm glad some in Moonlally remember her! The servants are too frightened to enter the old palace at night – which suits me. I can work away on my inventions without them bothering me.' He gulped the last of his tea and stood up. 'Come, I'll show you one of the wonders I'm known for. Moonlally's Magnificent Elephant – Model 10.'

Minou followed him to the line of hulking shapes under white canvas covers. Surely Shri had to be the rebel in the palace, the one Farisht had spoken of? He was certainly no friend of the General's. How clever she was, to have found him so quickly.

The clockmaker pulled the cloth back with a flourish. 'Look at this. Moonlally's Magnificent Mechanical Elephant 10 – the MMME 10 or *Thunderbolt*, as I've named her.'

'She's beautiful! Can I ride her?'

'Not this particular model, although my hunting elephants – the MMME 8s, or *Shikaras*, are designed to be ridden. You operate the *Thunderbolt* inside, look.'

He opened a door in the elephant's flank to reveal a compartment for the operator. 'Turn the wheel to steer and pull the lever to brake. Those pedals power her wheels. Powder and fuse here – these are elephant cannons, you see. Guns, in other words. The General has demanded a twenty-one-gun salute to mark Miss Ophelia's marriage.'

'Elephant cannons!' Minou reached up to pat the elephant's polished head. 'But they're made of wood. Why don't they catch fire?'

'Lined with steel,' Shri turned to Minou, his black eyes bright as a bird. 'It's late. Shouldn't you return to your quarters?'

Minou shivered. 'I would, but that mechanical at the gate nearly chopped my head off with his axe. He might get me on the way back.'

'Well, I invented every guard in this palace. I'll take care of him for you. Now, where are my tools…'

As they walked through the Lady's temple, Minou paused to fold her hands and bow to the Dark Lady. Shri nodded approvingly.

'I'm pleased to see you respect the Dark Lady,' he remarked. 'The General threw her out. Like the Whitetowners, he calls her a heathen idol. The workmen building his new fortress brought her to me and I built this little temple.'

'It's perfect. But what happened to her third eye – the black diamond of Moonlally?'

Shri shook his head. 'No one knows. But I'll tell you this – her third eye disappeared the day the young queen left the palace.'

Minou frowned. 'You mean – the day she *died*?'

Shri coughed. 'Yes, exactly.' He beckoned her out of the temple and began striding across the courtyard. 'The Dark Lady's spirit will not rest until her third eye is restored. The black diamond is a fallen star that protects Moonlally. I'm sure you've noticed the river is rising. A flood's due soon – it's almost thirteen years since the last one. The Lady's powers are returning.'

Minou tried to keep up, but she had no idea what the old clockmaker was talking about. When they reached her terrace gate, Shri unrolled a toolkit with all kinds of intricate attachments. He undid the pincer from the steel cap on his right wrist, clicked a screwdriver on to it, then levered the guard's helmet open and fiddled with the mechanism underneath.

'There! That should do it.' He nodded with satisfaction, as the mechanical wheeled slowly back and the gate swung open. 'You won't have any trouble now, Shadow. What did you say your name was?'

'Sparrow!' Minou slipped through the gate and turned to him. 'Thank you. I'm glad we met, Shri. I'd love to try out those batwings – if you need help with your inventions.'

The man chuckled. 'Are you sure you're brave enough?'

'Of course! But it'll have to be soon. Before I'm sent to Lutetia for Miss Ophelia's wedding.' She looked at Shri wonderingly. He had to be the rebel in the palace, and who knew if she'd ever see him again? She decided to speak. 'Shri? Do you know of a flower called the green orchid? I was told they grew inside the palace.'

'Hmm.' The old man looked at her with piercing eyes. 'Can't say I have, child,' he muttered. 'Botany's not my strong point. I'm an engineer myself.' He glanced back at the courtyard suspiciously and lowered his voice to a whisper. 'But I do know someone with an interest in that flower. She's the only other soul in Moonlally who knows the Queen's alive!'

'*Alive!* Do you really mean it?' Minou gasped. 'But... but everybody knows the Queen's dead – there was a funeral – Dima took me. I was a tiny baby strapped to her chest.'

'Well, I can't swear to it. But I tell you this. The young queen was not buried that day. It was a false funeral.'

'How do you know?'

'Who do you think made the wax effigy they placed in her casket?'

'Um... you?'

'Who else? I hoped she'd escaped the General and fled Moonlally, taking the third eye with her as protection. I knew she'd be safer if everyone believed she was dead, so I agreed to do as the General asked.'

He fished something from his toolkit and slipped it quickly through the barred gate, pressing it into Minou's hand. 'This skeleton key opens your gate. Come to my workshop tomorrow night. I'll introduce you. Until then, may the Dark Lady be with you.'

'And with you, Shri.' Minou watched the old man shuffle across the courtyard until he faded into moonlight and shadow. Could the Queen truly be alive? Or had the years he'd spent locked away in the palace confused the poor clockmaker? She looked down at the worn iron key in her hand.

There was only one way to find out.

Fifteen

Thrilled though she was with all she'd discovered, Minou was so tired after her night exploring, she could barely stay awake for her geometry lesson the next day.

'I despair, child. You have yawned all morning, and your complexion is quite grey.' Mamzelle shook her head. 'But your frocks are back from the dressmaker, let's see if they fit. And then, perhaps a deportment lesson will wake you up?'

Suddenly alert, Minou sprang to her feet to follow Mamzelle upstairs, remembering the painted sparrow she'd slipped into the ballgown. She hoped Jay had found it and sent her a message in reply.

In the bedchamber, the governess opened the trunk and lifted out the top garment, folded in tissue paper. 'Let's begin with the blue day dress. If that fits, we don't need to bother with the others.'

'But what about the ballgown, Mamzelle? Don't you think I should try that too? And my slippers will have heels – the length must be perfect.'

'True. And you may keep the long gown on. Today, I will teach you to curtsey.'

While she tried the dress on, Minou checked the hem for a rustle of paper but found nothing. Someone had taken out her painted sparrow but hadn't sent a reply. She sighed, disappointed. 'I already know how to curtsey, Mamzelle.'

'You will not be familiar with the full curtsey, for royalty. Slide your right foot from fourth to second position and bend your knees as you descend.'

Minou attempted an awkward dip, the corset digging painfully into her belly.

'Knees forward! Don't stick out your behind. Once more, with a weight balanced on your head – ah, this will do!' Mamzelle opened the window seat and lifted out a hefty, leatherbound volume of fairy tales.

'Really, Mamzelle?' Minou winced as the heavy book was placed on the crown of her head. 'I have a headache—'

'We must perfect your posture – the *Napoleon* departs for Lutetia soon. *Child!*'

At this news, Minou jerked her head and sent the book sliding to the ground. 'Sorry! How soon, exactly, Mamzelle?'

'Tomorrow or the day after – depending on weather conditions.'

'Tomorrow!' Minou was suddenly dizzy. 'As soon as that! Mamzelle, I don't feel well – may I take the gown off? It's this corset, I can hardly breathe.'

'Nonsense. I'll tighten the strings – you'll feel an improvement.' Mamzelle winched the corset in so tight that Minou felt blood drain from her face.

'Ouch! It hurts, Mamzelle,' she exclaimed, slumping on to the padded window seat.

'Goodness, child, you've turned quite pale! Take off the ballgown – we can't have you make a mess of it.'

Mamzelle lifted the ballgown over Minou's head and loosened her corset strings. 'I'll bring water!' she called as she clattered to the sink.

Minou would never get used to that awful corset. No wonder Whitetown ladies were always swooning – it was a miracle any blood reached their heads at all. She gazed up at the sky-blue ceiling, painted with kingfishers, parakeets and doves. Golden lines arched over the dome to the centre. How had she not seen it before? The ceiling of the young queen's bedroom was painted to look like a birdcage. Had she been locked away by the General in this very room? Minou felt queasy at the thought.

She glanced down at the book of fairy tales, fallen open at a story called *The Runaway Princess*. It had once belonged to the young queen – who was not dead, according to Shri. She hoped to meet the Green Orchid tonight, as he'd promised. There was so little time before she left for Lutetia.

Mamzelle excused Minou from afternoon lessons, which meant she was left restlessly pacing her chamber. As dusk fell, she took the skeleton key from her pocket and threw the black silk tunic over her petticoats. She tiptoed on to her terrace and peered through the iron gate into the courtyard, to check the coast was clear. There was the servant girl, a slim white figure, darting towards the elephant stables. This time, Minou would catch her.

The skeleton key was worn, but with a little fumbling, it turned stiffly in the lock. She eyed the mechanical guard as he slid forward. But the gate swung safely open and Minou hurried through, letting out a breath. Now she had to find the girl. She set off swiftly, retracing her steps from the night before.

There was no one at the elephant stables, although the animals had been fed; purple figs were strewn on the ground. Minou reached over the half-door of the stable to pat the great creature and felt a damp kiss on her forehead – the same elephant she'd spoken to yesterday, delicately extending its trunk. She felt a pang at the touch. It reminded her how Dima would anoint her forehead with red powder after morning prayers. Her eyes stung with tears. At once, she was back in their tumbledown shack. She could almost feel the rough criss-cross ropes of her hammock and sniff the tobacco smoke of her grandmother's pipe.

She swiped at her face. What was the use of thinking about it? Her old life was gone now. Dima lay cold in her tomb and the ashes of their home had washed away on the flowing river. And Tal and Little were still missing. Minou had been in the palace for days and hadn't found the Green Orchid. She was determined to do as Jay had said, but she hadn't made a good cobra so far.

Sighing, she turned to climb the stairs to the stable roof, skirting round to the platform, from where she'd had a good view before. The servant girl was easy to spot in her white tunic and trousers. She stood by the gates, talking to Shri. Minou watched them gesture and point at the General's fortress. If the clockmaker knew the servant girl, surely she must be the rebel Farisht had mentioned? She'd let them finish talking and slip into the workshop.

She tiptoed down and pushed open the green door of the Dark Lady's temple. The coloured lights cast a soft radiance over the icon. Minou lowered her head, touching the warmth of the tin elephant at her throat as she recited her names. *Cloudborn, Rainmaker, Lightning striker, Tide-turner, Moon dazzler, Storm summoner, Pearl finder, Sorrow healer, Song weaver.*

Most of the Dark Lady's names came easily to her now, but Minou wished she could recall the hymn Dima had sung under her breath as she circled the incense burner. If she ever escaped the palace, she'd ask Jay to teach her.

As she entered Shri's workshop, she saw a pair of batwings folded alongside the heap of mattresses. Idly, she pulled one wing open. Wouldn't it be fun to try them – to fly like a bird or glide like a bat! These wings took Shri's weight, so they could manage hers. And if she was going to try, it was now or never. A moment later, she'd looped the padded harness over her head and was tightening the straps around her waist. Shri was a small man and the harness fitted her snugly. But she needed to hurry – before he returned.

The batwings dragged on the floor, as she made her way to the ladder leading to the metal platform under the ceiling. She gripped its rungs firmly and climbed, remembering the words she'd heard Shri yell when he dived, like a large and skinny dragonfly. *Arms wide, knees bent.* She reached the platform and crawled over to crouch at the edge, trying not to look down. In the rafters above, bats rustled their wings, their red eyes glinting.

Minou stood, keeping her knees bent. Spanning her arms wide, she felt the metal spokes click into place. 'May the Dark Lady be with me,' she whispered.

The vast black wings fanned wide, making her teeter. As she plunged forward, they billowed out and she soared down into the warehouse. She landed with a crash on the pile of mattresses, bounced and then jolted into a somersault. Dazed, she found herself on her back, staring at the astonished faces of Shri and the servant girl.

Sixteen

'**O**uch!'

'Goodness! Is she dead?' the girl was saying.

'I heard her say *ouch*,' Shri pointed out.

'I'm fine!' Minou crowed, scrambling upright, her shoulders wrenched painfully backwards by the wings. She was dizzy, bruised and half-strangled by the harness, but alive.

'You gave us a fright!' The servant girl knelt to help Minou out of the harness.

'I hope you haven't torn my wings,' Shri tutted as he lifted them over her head. 'Not a bad first attempt. You're small, which aids the aerodynamics.'

The servant girl helped Shri lift the batwings and fold them away. She'd thrown back her white veil, wiry curls of hair escaping to frame her forehead. Minou blinked, rubbing her eyes. The girl's oval face and straight nose seemed strangely familiar, as did the brown eyes fixed on her.

'Are you sure you're all right, Sparrow?' the girl asked, smiling.

'How do you know my name?'

'Shri told me. And there's this.' The girl waved a scrap of paper, creased and slightly torn. Minou took it from her.

'My painted sparrow!' she exclaimed. 'Where did you find it?' It was her own watercolour – the one she'd hidden in the ballgown. But someone had added to it. Even in the gloom of the warehouse, Minou could see the sparrow held a tiny green flower in its beak. A green orchid! She looked up to see the girl pull a silver chain from under her tunic, an enamelled green flower strung upon it.

'See – you can trust me, Sparrow! *We have no hands, no face, no voice...*'

'*Like the Lady we thrive in darkness,*' Minou whispered. 'Farisht, the graveyard poet, said there was a rebel in the palace. I've found you!'

'Farisht – is that his name? I only know him as the poet. I haven't had a message from him in ages. And he's never sent a drawing before.'

'That's my drawing – not Farisht's,' Minou told her. 'I sent it to Jay, another of the rebels. His mother's the palace seamstress – slaving away with her three daughters to sew Miss Ophelia's fancy dresses. I slid it into the hem of the ballgown Mamzelle sent to be altered.'

'That awful trousseau!' the girl sighed. A look of surprise came over her face. 'Wait – you don't know who I am, do you?'

Minou nodded. 'Yes, I do. You're a palace servant. One who's not afraid of ghosts. Or crocodiles.'

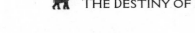

The servant girl laughed in delight. 'You've been watching me! What else have you noticed?'

'Well, I think your job is to feed the elephants. And you're a friend of Shri's, so I know you must be all right.'

The girl laughed again. 'My darling elephants! I do like to give them treats.'

'Sparrow, you know this is—' Shri began.

'Wait, Shri!' the girl interrupted. 'I want to tell Sparrow myself. We need a mirror; you must have one somewhere in this cavern of wonders?'

'What would an old man like me want with mirrors? But I believe there's one on that old almirah in the corner.'

'Come, Sparrow – over here!'

Minou followed her to the corner of the warehouse where a battered wooden almirah stood, shelves groaning with coils of wire and bolts of oilcloth. The servant girl wiped its dusty mirror clean with her sleeve.

'Look at us, Sparrow. Side by side.'

Minou reached out a hand to touch her face, mirrored in the silver glass. She stared at the girl's reflection and the girl stared back. The two were so alike they might have been twins. The girl was a head taller, with a sturdier build and Minou's nose turned up at the tip, but that was all.

'I'm Ophelia,' the servant girl said. 'Can't you tell?'

Minou's heart thudded with shock. Farisht had known there was a rebel in the palace, but he'd never guessed it was the General's own daughter! Miss Ophelia was the reason she was trapped here. Was she really a Green Orchid? She lowered her gaze, knowing she ought to be cautious. 'Miss Ophelia, I spoke out of turn. Did you know I was brought here as your Shadow?'

Ophelia shook her head. 'I had no idea until Mamzelle told me. I'm so sorry, Sparrow, for the way you were captured, and for the terrible things my father has done. But I'm on your side – the *rebels'* side! I have important information for them.'

Minou swallowed. 'What is it?' she asked. 'And excuse me, but why would they trust your information?'

'Hear me out, Sparrow,' Ophelia pleaded. 'I know you must find it hard to believe the General's daughter, but I have news that could lead to his downfall. The young queen is alive. She's in exile – and I know where!'

Minou's mouth fell open. 'How?' she whispered. 'How do you know all this?'

'I heard my father and my uncle, the Commandant, talking after my engagement to the Baron,' Ophelia told her. 'Thirteen years ago, on the night of the great storm, the young queen fled the palace. They sent spies to neighbouring kingdoms but found no trace of her. It suited them to claim she was dead, so the General might seize the queendom.'

'But if the Queen's alive – he has no right to the throne.'

'Exactly. And I won't have to marry that terrible baron. They say he murdered his first wife for her fortune. A regular Bluebeard!'

'But why would your father make you marry a murderer?'

The General's daughter sighed. 'He's quite mad. And the Commandant cares only for power. Our small colony marrying Lutetian nobility serves him well.'

Minou's head spun. She whirled round, turning to Shri in confusion.

'You can trust Miss Ophelia, Sparrow,' the old man reassured her. 'She's speaking the truth. This meeting between you was fated to happen.'

Minou gazed at Ophelia's face – a face so like her own, she felt the other girl might read the thoughts tumbling through her mind. 'I do,' she found herself saying. 'I do trust her.'

'Good. There is more we need to talk about, but it's late. Sparrow, you must return to your quarters and Ophelia to the fortress,' Shri added.

'But – wait.' Minou turned to Ophelia, remembering. 'Have you heard about two boys? They were arrested for throwing paint on the General's statue – Tal and Little. No one in Blacktown knows where they are.'

The General's daughter nodded. 'I have heard about those two', she said and sang—

'Two boys are missing.
They rouged the face
Of the General's statue
In Cathedral Place.
No mothers wept for them.
The police didn't care.
Two children, vanished
Into the night air.'

'That sounds like one of Farisht's songs! Do you know where they've been taken?' Minou asked impatiently.

The General's daughter shook her head. 'No. But I'll find out, I promise. Shri's right, it's late. You should return to your quarters. I'll come and find you tomorrow.'

'But what about the *Napoleon*? Mamzelle said it was due to depart tomorrow.'

'There's a sea mist over Moonlally Bay that isn't lifting. But we must be careful, Sparrow, Mamzelle cannot know we've met. Don't breathe a word, but play your part – until we meet again!'

Seventeen

After the night's excitement, Minou found lessons the following day terribly dull. Especially as Mamzelle was determined to tackle history. She'd enjoyed history lessons at Master Karu's, sitting in the dusty schoolyard to hear the daring exploits of Moonlally's queens. There was Queen Amani who'd ridden into battle standing on an elephant, Queen Leela who'd raised an orphaned tiger cub in the palace, and Queen Tara, who dived so deep for pearls in Moonlally Bay, she was rumoured to be part-mermaid. But the history of Lutetia that Mamzelle taught was very different. She had to memorise a list of Lutetian rulers as long as her arm.

'Once more, Mignon!'

Minou sighed. 'Clovis, Theuderic I, Theudebert I, Theudebald, Chlodomer, Childebert I, what's-his-name? Sorry, Mamzelle.'

She wondered if Ophelia learned the same lessons. If so, how would the General's daughter govern

Moonlally, knowing nothing of the Dark Lady or the history of the queendom? She asked Mamzelle, but the governess only sniffed.

'The General's daughter is not required to know foolish stories. Anyhow, like the General, she won't involve herself in day-to-day rule. The Commandant handles practical matters: which teak forest is for cutting, how much ivory to be harvested per elephant, when to raise the tax on tea and so on. It is more important that Ophelia – and you as her Shadow – impress the Baron with a knowledge of Lutetia's history.'

Minou frowned. 'But Lutetia is thousands of miles away, Mamzelle. How does its history matter?'

'Four thousand nine hundred and sixty-four miles, child. Dear me – have I taught you nothing? On the *Napoleon* the voyage is a full ten days, closer to twenty by steamship.'

'You mean the *Napoleon* travels at...' Minou calculated quickly, 'four hundred and ninety-six... five hundred miles a day?'

'Exactly. What an adventure! To float above the citadels of the north, crest snowy Himalayan peaks and cross desert sands, all before you arrive in the wonderful city of Lutetia. You will depart tomorrow, providing the sea mist lifts.'

Minou gulped. Tomorrow! How would she pass on whatever information Ophelia had about the Queen? She could do nothing from distant Lutetia. Both girls – Minou and Ophelia – were trapped in the palace like two birds in a cage.

She prowled her chamber restlessly, waiting for darkness. At dusk, she heard a knock at her door. Before she could answer, Ophelia entered in her servant girl garb, carrying a bundle of clothing. Closing the door softly behind her, she threw back her veil and whispered.

'Come, Sparrow – we must be quick!' She handed Minou the bundle. 'A set of maid's clothes, like mine. Put them on!'

Minou took the tunic, trousers and white veil. 'Where are we going?'

'I have to show you something,' the General's daughter whispered. 'We'll be safer dressed like this.'

They hurried out of the chamber and into the old palace. As they approached the elephant stables, the huge animals trumpeted.

'Quiet, girls!' Ophelia whispered. 'Would you like to feed them, Sparrow? Figs are their favourite.' She took a handful of purple figs from her pocket for Minou. The creatures uncurled their trunks and plucked them from her hand. Minou stroked the trunk of the largest elephant, who harrumphed happily in reply, as if she recognised her.

'I met you the other night, didn't I?' she whispered.

'That's Claudette. She's the matriarch. The others are Bernadine, Gigi and Fleur. I feed them every night,' Ophelia told Minou. 'I'm not supposed to, not after my engagement to the Baron. But I missed them! So, I dressed in the maid's clothes and crept out secretly. One night, I heard banging – that's how I found Shri in his workshop. But we must be silent – I'll tell you later. Come on!'

They had come to the iron gates that led to the inner part of the palace. 'We'll cross to the fortress,' Ophelia whispered. 'Follow me and don't say a word. If anyone stops us, I'll do the talking.'

She unlocked a small gate set within a larger one and led them through. Minou knew, from Dima's tales, that avenues of palm trees and lush gardens of tropical flowers once surrounded the Temple of the Dark Lady. Now there was only a stark expanse of stone paving with a wide path, picked out in gold, leading to the castle. Servants hurried across the space: men dressed in white with purple turbans and veiled women in the white tunics that she and Ophelia wore. Luckily, no one gave them a second glance.

As they approached the bridge, Minou stared up at the vast grey castle before them. A tower stood at each corner, flying the General's purple flag. Mechanical guards flanked the arched wooden doors, their reflections mirrored in the flat silver of the moat. The *moat!* She glanced at it as she followed Ophelia over the bridge, remembering Mamzelle's threat and the crocodiles she'd spotted from the stable roof.

'We'll go through the servants' entrance. It's a bit of a climb to my chamber,' Ophelia hissed, as she followed her over the bridge and around the castle walls.

They tiptoed past a wide doorway to the kitchens, bustling with activity, though it was late.

A blood-curdling scream rang from a high window above, echoing into the night.

'What was that noise?' Minou gulped. 'Is someone being fed to the crocodiles?'

'No, no – that was my mother,' Ophelia whispered, pulling her past the kitchens. 'I expect her bathwater wasn't the right temperature or her coffee lacked enough cream. This way!' The girl opened a small door and Minou followed her up a spiral staircase into the tower room.

'By the Lady! What's that *smell*?' she asked.

Ophelia laughed and pulled her inside. 'Bats!' she said simply. 'Don't worry – they reek, but they're friendly!'

If Minou had tried to picture the General's daughter's apartment, she could not have imagined the scene before her. The whole of Ophelia's round tower room, with its bare stone floor and white walls, had been given to the bats. Bats roosted in the rafters, bats flitted over the floor, strewn with straw and scattered droppings. Bowls of fruit and water were set upon a wooden table for the pampered creatures. Shri's workshop was so vast Minou had only noticed a slight mustiness but here, she had to pinch her nose.

'I sleep in a side room – less stinky,' Ophelia told her, leading Minou into a space that might have been a dressing room. It contained a narrow white bed and a pile of leatherbound books on a table. The window was propped open, a large almirah occupied one wall.

'This is what I need to show you, Sparrow. Look!' Ophelia unlocked the wardrobe and flung open the doors. Pasted inside were hundreds of tiny pieces of paper, each in the same handwriting. Minou stared at the yellowing scraps, tracing them with her fingertips as she read the words. 'But these are Farisht's poems!' she exclaimed, reading,

> *'You ask why I write dark words*
> *that take wing by veiled night.*
> *Friends, words you dare not speak,*
> *the poets alone dare write.'*

'That's how I became a Green Orchid. Because of the poet. The bats bring me his words – just as they brought your painting of a sparrow.'

'Two boys,' Minou whispered. Papered inside Ophelia's wardrobe was the story of Tal and Little. She turned to her. 'Did you find out where they are?'

Ophelia shook her head. 'But I know they're not in the palace, Sparrow. One of the cooks said they'd been taken on a hunt. To act as bearers, I expect.'

'What about the crocodiles? Surely the General doesn't really feed prisoners to those creatures?'

The General's daughter winced; her face stricken. 'He has done. But they haven't held one of his horrible executions for a while. The boys are safe.'

Minou stepped back in horror. 'So, it's *true*! How can you stand it?'

'The truth is, I can't, Sparrow. I didn't know. I lived with Mamzelle, away from the General and my mother. One night, I didn't drink the milk she'd left for me. Later, I found out it was drugged, so I'd sleep through the awful sounds. I wandered on to the moonlit roof and saw it—' Ophelia covered her face with her hands.

'Saw what?'

'The execution. It was horrible – the churning water and that poor man's screams! I asked to move to this deserted tower alone. I've always loved animals – so I allowed the bats to keep roosting here. Which has the advantage of keeping Mamzelle from snooping – she's terrified of them. One evening, a bat dropped a slip of paper with a scrap of verse from the poet. I sent a note in reply and learned of the rebels working to overthrow my father. To the poet, my codename was the Batkeeper. I couldn't tell him who I really was.'

'After the Commandant arranged my engagement to the Baron, lessons with Mamzelle stopped and I was told to stay in my chamber. I wasn't having that. I started slipping out at night in servants' clothes and met Shri. I was allowed to visit Father Jacob for spiritual instruction and he told me—'

'Of course – I saw you!' Minou cried. 'That Sunday by the Lally, in the Commandant's carriage. The day the *Napoleon* caught fire.'

Ophelia's eyes widened. 'Yes! I was returning from a visit to Father Jacob. You were staring in at the carriage window – I remember thinking you looked familiar, like a long-lost little sister!' She took a step forward. 'Sparrow, I have something of vital importance to the rebels – the place where the Queen is living in exile. Now you're here, we must pass the map to the Green Orchids.'

'You have a map?'

'Yes, it's hidden in the Dark Lady's temple. I want to give it to the poet. But how do we get it to him?'

'Can't you send it with the bats?'

'Too dangerous – what if it falls into the wrong hands? We'd put the Queen's life in danger.'

Minou frowned. She was as much a prisoner as Ophelia. On board the airship she'd be watched closely by the Shadow General and Wife as well as the crew… The crew – that was it!

'I have an idea. Could you ask for someone to join the *Napoleon*? He's the son of the palace dressmaker.'

'Your friend? The one who drew a green orchid in the sparrow's beak?'

'Jay would be perfect. He's a trained navigator and a skilled kalari fighter.'

Ophelia nodded. 'That's a marvellous idea. I'll ask for him to join as reward for his mother's long service. You can give him the map on the *Napoleon*. But how will he return to Moonlally and tell the other rebels?'

Minou hadn't thought of that. At the speed the airship travelled, Jay would be hundreds of miles away by the time it made its first stop.

She frowned. 'I'll think of something. Let's talk tomorrow night at Shri's workshop. Unless we're too late – Mamzelle said the *Napoleon* leaves in the morning?'

'The forecast is that the mist won't lift for a day or so. Shri's workshop – at midnight.' Ophelia took Minou's hand. 'I'm so glad we found each other. When I saw that painted sparrow with a green orchid, I knew it meant hope – at last!'

Eighteen

Mamzelle was busy with preparations for the voyage the following day, which left Minou time to work out her plan. She'd decided to escape the *Napoleon* with Jay – she had no wish to be sent to Lutetia. This way, they'd return to Moonlally together and give Farisht the map. She'd show Jay how to think like a cobra – by fleeing the palace right under the General's nose!

She flitted about her chamber like a caged bird, eager to share her idea, until she heard the water clock strike its brassy midnight note. Bats swooped from the sky as she stole on to the terrace. She used the skeleton key to unlock her gate, and no longer flinched at the huge mechanical, cranking forward to open it.

Slipping silently into the courtyard, she made for the Temple of the Dark Lady, pausing to bow and whisper the Lady's thirteen names, ending with *Elephant tamer, Flood bringer, Green sower, Queen crowner.*

The tin elephant pulsed at her throat like a tiny heart and Minou felt a glow within her. She was helping to do what Dima had dreamed of: restore the queendom. Having paid her respects, she pushed the warehouse doors open. Shri and Ophelia turned to her expectantly.

'Sparrow!' Ophelia called. 'I've been telling Shri our plans. Jay will be on board the *Napoleon* as junior navigator. I've arranged everything.'

'Not a bad idea. But how is that boy going to get back to Moonlally?' Shri shook his head. 'The airship won't refuel until it's hundreds of miles north of here.'

'I have an even better plan.'

'Well?' Ophelia gave a little clap of impatience. 'What is it?'

'Jay and I will leave the airship as soon as it takes flight. We'll return to Moonlally together and give the map to Farisht.'

'How?'

Minou pointed to the batwings, folded beside the heap of mattresses. 'With those. That's what they're for, isn't it, Shri? To evacuate the airship in an emergency.'

'But of course!' Ophelia slapped her forehead. 'I've watched you jump myself. Why didn't I think of that? And your friend—'

'Jay's a trained navigator. He'll guide us back to Moonlally from wherever we land. There might not be time to explain everything on board, but he trusts me.'

'Well, for safety's sake, I insist you jump out over water,' Shri added. 'You're lucky Moonlally Bay doesn't have too many sharks at this time of year. The batwing harnesses are stuffed with kapok – so you'll float. You'll find the emergency equipment down in the *Napoleon*'s hold, next to the hatch.'

Ophelia frowned. 'But what happens when the crew find you've escaped? Bother it, by the time they do, you'll be long gone.' She seized Minou's hand. 'It's a marvellous idea. Come, Sparrow – I'll give you the map.'

Under the coloured lights of the temple, Shri bowed to the Dark Lady, then kneeled to unscrew a panel from the base of her plinth. He pulled out a scroll tied with green ribbon. Ophelia crouched and spread it open on the floor.

'While Queen Ambra was locked in the palace,' she explained, 'Shri told me that she wrote in secret to a friend – her only visitor. I managed to get hold of her letters. She told him how she longed to escape and live with the nuns in the hills. And she drew this map, so he could find her – after she'd fled Moonlally.'

Minou's gaze traced the lines of the map, delicately painted in watercolour. In the hills beyond Moonlally, on a natural plateau, stood the famous temple at Narsin, its pink marble carved with images of the old gods. An arrow pointed to a scattering of small white shrines, dotting the blue peaks beyond.

'An order of nuns lives among those old shrines. The Queen planned to take refuge with them. It's supposed to be the place where the Dark Lady once prayed to the gods for a daughter and heir.'

'And now, we must ask the Dark Lady for her blessing,' Shri told them. 'Dark Lady of Moonlally, we pray for protection. Almost thirteen years have passed since the river last flooded. Your power grows. When our queen is restored and the General overthrown, your temple will rise from the ruins of his fortress. Moonlally will bathe in the radiance of your third eye once more.' He began to chant. With a pang, Minou recognised the hymn to the Dark Lady that Dima sung each morning at her altar.

'Dark Lady, born of the clouded hills,
whose songs summon the rains down still,
whose third eye spears in lightning strike,
whose powers turn back the highest tide.
Your radiance rivals the silver moon,
your anger brings tempest with monsoon.
Grant us blessings as pearls from oceans deep.
May your amber gaze heal those that weep.
Beloved of poets, weavers of words,
your soft voice tames wild elephant herds.
When the floodwaters rise at year thirteen,
to renew red earth and clothe her green,
then anoint our queendom's rightful queen.'

The girls kneeled before the Dark Lady. Minou gazed at the beautiful face of the icon, and the empty hollow of her perfect forehead. She thought of Dima, kneeling to pray before the Dark Lady every morning, and how carelessly Dima's killers had smashed the icon into fragments of clay. Surely the Dark Lady would help them?

But there was so much that might go wrong. What if the batwings failed and she and Jay plummeted to their deaths? Or the Queen was no longer in exile in the hills? And hadn't Shri said that the Dark Lady's third eye protected the queendom – suppose the Queen no longer had the diamond? Shaking off her worries, she closed her eyes and murmured her own private prayer.

Dark Lady, I promise to help restore the queendom. For my Dima.

Ophelia rolled up the map and handed it to Minou. 'Hide it well, Sparrow!'

Minou took it from her. 'But, Ophelia, what about you?' she asked. 'They'll take you to Lutetia on a steamship and force you to marry the Baron.'

Ophelia made a face. 'As if I'd marry that Bluebeard! Leaving Moonlally gives me a chance to slip free of the palace once and for all. Mamzelle has lots of potions up her sleeve. I'll find a way to return and join the rebels – and restore our rightful queen.'

She stepped forward to hug Minou. 'May the Dark Lady be with you, Sparrow. Good luck!'

Minou smiled at the face that so resembled her own. 'May the Lady's blessings fall upon us all,' she said.

With the task that lay ahead, they needed her.

Nineteen

The following morning, the *Napoleon* took flight. Minou dressed carefully: lacing her boots tight and pinning her hair under her straw hat with its lace veil. She slid the map, rolled in oilcloth, into her left boot and tucked the tin elephant safely under her collar.

Mamzelle escorted her to the palace gates as a sleek motorcar drew up. 'The General has sixteen motorcars, Mignon – this is a new model, I believe. It has electric lights and glass windows.' The car was black and shiny as a cockroach – far superior to Father Jacob's battered green jalopy, the only other motor Minou had seen up close. But what use did the General have for it, she wondered, if he never left the palace?

They settled inside, the chauffeur driving at a stately pace over the bridge and along the road to the Moonlally shore. Two riders on horseback accompanied them through the city, one hoisting the General's purple flag, the other blowing a bugle to clear the road of bicycles and stray animals. Minou gazed out of the window at the familiar sights – the wide green river, Blacktowners walking dusty roads to jobs at factories or Whitetown villas. Soon, she'd be free to wander the streets of Moonlally again.

As they approached the seashore, she saw the giant hangar where the *Napoleon* was kept, its mooring mast rising into the sky. Minou craned her neck out of the window to gaze upwards. The *Napoleon* floated like a giant purple cloud, the air vibrating with the deafening rumble of its engines. It reminded her of a thunder god's chariot from the old tales.

Under the airship's black shadow, Minou followed Mamzelle to the mooring mast. Thrilled as she was to be free of the palace, she felt a flutter of nerves beneath her ribs at the thought of jumping from such a height. Above them, the great balloon strained at its tethers; its huge ropes, wide as a man's arm, creaking and groaning in the blustering wind.

Mamzelle marched her to the foot of the mast and tugged at a bell. 'Thank goodness this wind has blown the sea mist away! Conditions clear for departure. Now, hop into the elevator, don't be afraid.'

A pair of barred doors slid open and they stepped into a metal cage that jerked slowly upwards. The elevator clanked to a halt, its doors screeched wide and a young man wearing a purple jacket bowed in greeting. 'Welcome on board, Miss *Ophelia*,' he announced.

Minou tried to hide her happiness, her heart leaping at the familiar voice. Her plan had worked – Jay was one of the *Napoleon*'s crew, just as Ophelia promised. She wanted to hug him but contented herself with a curtsey.

'I had expected the captain to greet us himself,' Mamzelle sniffed. 'But no matter. Go with this young man – he will show you to your cabin. I must hurry down to escort your, er, parents to the elevator. Look, they've arrived.'

Curious, Minou followed Mamzelle's gaze to the ground. Two figures emerged from an even larger black car: a man in uniform and a tall woman clutching her hat. They had to be the Shadow General and Wife.

'This way, Miss Ophelia.' Jay guided her along a clanking metal gangway that led to the door of the airship.

'Jay, don't you recognise me? *We have no hands, no face, no voice…*' Minou whispered, worried Jay hadn't known her under her veil.

'*Like the Lady, we thrive in darkness,*' Jay whispered back. 'Of course, Sparrow – but I didn't want to let on! This is the passenger deck, Miss Ophelia,' he added loudly as they entered the airship's gondola and were greeted by other crew members. 'Your cabin is on the left.' He indicated a wood-panelled passage lined with doors. 'I'll show you to the viewing lounge.'

Minou followed him to a spiral staircase that twisted down to another level of the gondola. The room had been fitted out as a vast lounge, carpeted in deep purple and dotted with cane chairs and palm trees. One wall was made entirely of glass. Through it, Minou could see a wash of turquoise bay below, with small figures of fishermen hauling their boats on to golden sand. A portrait of the General scowled from the wall, his black eyes glaring from a powdered face.

'Jay, I have to tell you about—'

The older boy raised a finger to his lips in warning, and Minou turned to see the Shadow General enter, accompanied by the Shadow Wife. He wore a purple naval jacket, breeches and a bicorne hat, his jowly face was made-up a chalky white and his handlebar moustache oiled.

Minou remembered Mamzelle's instructions and lurched into an abrupt curtsey. 'Mama, Papa.'

The Shadow General only frowned, but his wife inclined her head in reply, 'Daughter.' The Shadow Wife's red hair was piled in an elaborate heap and her powdered face perfectly blank. 'One hopes the voyage is pleasant,' she added, her tone less screechy than the voice Minou had heard in the palace.

She tried not to giggle. Jay caught her eye. 'Er – with your permission, General,' he said. 'May I escort Miss Ophelia to the flight deck below? Captain wondered if she'd like to see our departure from the helm.'

'Proceed!' the Shadow General barked, banging his cane on the floor as the Shadow Wife waved a careless, white-gloved hand.

Minou followed Jay down another flight of stairs to a room hung with maps and dotted with instruments. Telescopes were stationed at the windows and the crew bustled about, making adjustments. The dusty ground looked very far away. She swallowed, realising how high they were – and they hadn't taken off yet. Gliding into the sea from the airship would be very different from her dive and crash-landing in Shri's warehouse.

The floor dipped beneath them as the balloon lurched in the breeze. Minou stumbled and Jay held out his arm to steady her. 'Sparrow! What's going on? I was summoned to join the crew with an official letter. I knew something was up – your painting of a sparrow was tucked inside.'

'There's no time to explain,' Minou whispered. 'We must be quick as lightning! I've sneaked about the palace like a cobra. You'd have been proud of me.'

'A *cobra*?'

'Spying,' Minou hissed. 'Like you said, remember? I have information. But first, we need to find the escape hatch. We're both jumping ship.'

'Jumping *ship*?' Jay nodded towards the stairs. 'The hatch is a level down, in the luggage hold. I'll show you – hurry, though. But what about the captain? He's invited you to stand at the helm to watch the ship take off.'

Minou followed Jay to a room piled with trunks and boxes. She pointed to the sets of batwings clipped to the wall. 'We'll use those to jump once we're over Moonlally Bay.'

'The gliders? I saw the crew use them to jump free when the airship caught fire. Looked all right.'

'Can you do it – you're not scared?'

'Absolutely not. I've trained as a paraglider. You?'

Minou grimaced. Her insides felt as coiled up and writhing as a snake. 'Maybe a little?' she told him truthfully. The airship engines thrummed a higher note.

Jay shrugged. 'Lucky there isn't time to worry – we're about to take off. I'll take you to the captain, or it'll look suspicious. Once we're over the water, join me here. We'll be at Moonlally Bay in minutes.'

Minou followed Jay to the front of the gondola, where the captain beckoned her to the helm. The *Napoleon* had been newly refurbished after the explosion, its interior shone with polished brass and varnished wood. She watched with interest as the crew flew about, manning rudders, checking dials and pulling levers. With much shouting and signalling, they uncoupled the clamp holding the airship's ropes to the mast. The deck jerked beneath her feet, as the great balloon tugged free to rise into the air. The *Napoleon* had taken flight.

'As smooth a departure as you're likely to see, Miss Ophelia,' the captain told her.

Minou peered through the glass, wishing she could lift her veil for a better view. 'Are we turning around, Captain?'

'We always take a lap of the city before heading out, miss.' He glanced at her. 'So the people may witness the *Napoleon*'s magnificence.'

'Of course.' Minou remembered Dima shaking her fist and cursing the airship. Looking down, she felt a pang at the sight of the Lally glittering in the morning sun. Curved and shiny as a blade, it sliced between Whitetown and the huddle of Blacktown. How she missed the river – it was the only home she'd ever known.

The *Napoleon* banked in a wide circle to pass over the palace. Below, Minou could see the queue of tradesmen at the gates, like a line of ants. The elephants parading the palace grounds, looked no bigger than children's toys. Their flight path drifted on, heading for the curve of Moonlally Bay and the sea beyond. She turned from the window hastily, remembering their plan.

'Are you all right, Miss Ophelia? You look a little pale.'

'Captain, please excuse me. I do feel rather unwell. I'll retire to my cabin – please tell the crew I'm not to be disturbed.'

She hurried through the navigation room, glancing about to see all were occupied as she tiptoed down to the hold.

'You're here!' Jay called above the low rumbling of the engines. 'Finally – I'll go first.' He strapped Minou into her harness and tightened his own. 'May the Lady be with us!' Wings trailing behind him, he pushed open the safety hatch, lowered the ladder and swung out, dangling below the gondola. A rush of fierce wind gusted through the cabin.

Minou gripped the bar above the hatch, her heart in her throat. 'Arms wide, knees bent and don't look down!' she yelled over the howling wind.

And then, he was gone.

She watched Jay drop like a stone until he managed to fling his arms wide with a yell. The great black wings billowed and filled with air, curving to slow his plummeting course as he swooped from view.

Jay was flying – really flying – on Shri's inventions, made of nothing more than silk and wire. But then, the *Napoleon*, with its furniture and fittings, its passengers and crew, was only held up by fabric and steel, inflated with an invisible gas, lighter than air.

A queasiness stirred in her belly as she gazed at the vast sea below, rippled with foamy white. It was her turn to jump. She tried not to think about the sharks in Moonlally Bay. At least she could swim – before she'd walked, according to Dima.

'May the Lady be with me,' she whispered and kissed the tin elephant for luck. Tucking it under her collar, she spread her arms wide and dived head first into blue air.

III

To the Hills

Queen Tara, Tiger Tamer

As a girl, Queen Leela found a sickly tiger cub abandoned in the forest and summoned doctors to save it. She fed it buffalo milk and let it sleep in her bed. Shankar the tiger grew to full-size, but stayed tame as a rabbit. Her mother insisted Shankar return to the forest and only allowed Leela to visit after a year had passed. Her ayah reported the astonishing sight of a full-grown tiger springing at her, then rolling on the ground to have its belly tickled.

From *A True History of the Queens of Moonlally*

Twenty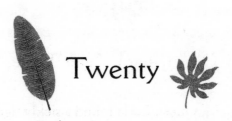

One of Dima's sayings was: *Don't ask the caterpillar how it feels to become a butterfly.* Which means, life rarely turns out as you expect.

And it was true. Jumping from the *Napoleon* was far more frightening than Minou had imagined. She plunged into free fall, air whistling past her ears, skirts ballooning around her. The batwings wrenched her arms painfully back as they domed open. The green water rushed closer at a terrifying speed. She could see white foam edging the waves and dark shapes moving below. She was going to drown! Or be eaten by sharks. Or both.

And then she remembered. *Arms wide, knees bent.* Her legs flailed as she struggled to pull them in against the buffeting wind. The tailpiece clicked; she felt a lift under her wings and relief as the harness straps eased. She was swooping through blue air, graceful as a hawk – '*Woohooo!*'

Until she landed, with a painful smack, face down in the sea. She surfaced, treading water, coughing and spluttering, her ears ringing from the rapid descent. The batwings trailed behind her. Tiny shoals of fish darted from her kicking legs. She tugged, struggling to free herself from the harness. Then she recalled why it was so bulky – Shri had stuffed it with kapok, for buoyancy. She was floating.

Minou rubbed her stinging face and scanned the horizon for Jay. He was nowhere to be seen. Eyes streaming and retching seawater, she splashed her way slowly to the beach, dragging herself on to the warm sand, where she collapsed, groaning with effort.

The shore was empty, but for a dilapidated fishing boat and a couple of cows, mooing mournfully. Minou sat up, unstrapping the harness and shrugging off her wings. She emptied her boots of water, checking the map was safe, and wrung out her soaked dress.

She stared out to sea. A white glare danced off the surface, foamy waves swelled and were calmed by the bay's curve. She could make out the *Napoleon* as a purple oval on the distant horizon, exactly the size and shape of an eggplant. She watched it grow smaller and smaller until it was no bigger than a grape. She'd done it. Escaped from the *Napoleon* – the General's own airship. But where was Jay? And how long did they have until the crew discovered they were missing?

She turned to look inland. The hazy outline of Moonlally flickered through the shimmering heat.

Scrambling up on to the sand dunes, she could see a black line snaking along the scrubby coastline. That must be the railway track – and there, coming towards her, was Jay.

'Sparrow!'

'By the Lady! Where did you go, Jay?'

'To scope out the terrain. We're near the railway line – we can follow it back to Moonlally. So, what's this information you have for the Green Orchids?'

Minou suppressed a smile at Jay's eager face as she took the map carefully from her boot. 'You might want to sit down,' she told him as she unfolded the paper with a flourish. 'Because I have a map in my possession. Not just any map. One showing the whereabouts of the Queen of Moonlally. She's *alive!*' She recounted the story as she'd heard it from Ophelia.

The boy shook his head in disbelief. 'Are you telling me the rebel in the palace is the General's daughter? How do we know this isn't a trap to smoke out the Green Orchids?'

'Ophelia's not a traitor, Jay. I've seen Farisht's poems papered over her almirah. The bats carry messages between the two of them.'

Jay frowned. 'I did hear Farisht was exchanging messages with a rebel in the palace, codenamed Batkeeper. But neither of us dreamed it was the General's daughter.'

'There you are. Farisht will vouch for her.'

'Now that's another thing. When you disappeared, I went to the cemetery to find you. But Farisht wasn't there. He hasn't been seen since the night of your Dima's funeral. His song for the General caused a sensation. I hear there's a warrant out for his arrest.'

'But you got my painting – the sparrow in the hem of Ophelia's ballgown?'

'Leena found it. I realised you were in the palace, though I couldn't work out how you'd got there. So, I drew the green orchid in its beak and went to the graveyard. Farisht was still missing, but I managed to get one of his flying mice to take it. Bit me, vicious thing!'

'That explains how it got to Ophelia. I know she's loyal to our cause, Jay. She even wears a green orchid necklace.'

Jay flopped on to the sand and stared up at the sky. 'We need to think about this. Let's say the Queen is alive. She left Moonlally years ago – she could be anywhere by now!'

'What are you saying?'

'This information's only a hunch. How do we know the Queen's still there?'

'But if there's a chance we might find her – however small – we must try! The rebels need someone to fight *for* as well as to fight against.'

Jay frowned. 'Thundering elephants! Sparrow, we can't expect people to risk their lives without evidence. Actual proof the Queen's alive.'

'Could we take the map to Karu?'

'My brother wouldn't leave his precious school on some wild goose chase,' Jay snorted. 'And Farisht's missing. He's the only one who'd do this.'

'No, he's not!' Minou jumped up in excitement. 'What about us? Why don't we take the map and find the Queen? Ophelia said it's a day's journey from Narsin.'

'Find the Queen ourselves – you and me?'

Minou nodded. 'We'll have the proof we need – and we can tell the other rebels.'

Jay pointed at the railway line. 'As it happens, the train to Samudra stops at Narsin. It passes through here. If we jump on board, we could be at the temple tomorrow morning.'

'Yes! But how do we get the train to stop? There's no station.'

Jay scratched his head. 'We could block the tracks to slow it down and sneak on board. Maybe drag a fallen palm tree on to the line? Let's see what we can find.'

Together, they scrambled up over the sand dunes and made their way towards the railway line. Minou took a deep breath of sea air. A dizzying lightness took hold of her – a heady freedom now she was no longer prisoner in the palace. She glanced back at the blue ocean, uneasily. The *Napoleon* was still visible as a speck on the horizon. What if they'd noticed she was missing, and were returning to find her? The sooner they were off this beach, the better.

'Hey!' Jay yelled. 'I don't believe it. Those creatures have eaten my wings.' The two cows were chewing away at his batwings, with more determination than pleasure. 'Shame they've ruined them – they're amazing inventions.' He slung Minou's harness over his head and lifted his arms to spread the black wings wide in the breeze.

'Jay, look at the cows!' Minou pointed at the horned beasts, backing away and mooing frantically at the sight. 'They're terrified. They think you're a huge bird – a vulture or something. What if we herd them on to the railway tracks, to make the train stop?'

'That's an idea!' Jay exclaimed. 'Wait here.' He dashed towards the boat and returned with a length of tangled fishing line. 'We'll rope them together. You take the ends and lead them to the track while I drive them on with the batwings–'

As they reached the railway line, cows in tow, Minou decided Jay had picked the better job. While he ran at them, batwings raised, she hung on to the roped beasts as they galloped away, yanked to the ground and dragged on her behind. When she complained, Jay grinned wickedly.

'Glad you're the same old Sparrow! Thought you might have developed airs and graces in the palace.'

Minou narrowed her eyes at him. She pointed to a distant line of smoke, spiralling in the still midday heat. 'Looks like the train's here.'

'By the Lady!' Jay dropped the rope. 'The Samudra Express is never on time.'

Minou glanced down at her dress. Her hem was tattered, the bodice slashed and every centimetre of white cotton was coated in dust or spattered with dung. Jay's purple and gold airman's jacket was just as dishevelled. 'But we're filthy. And we haven't got money, or train tickets.'

'We don't need tickets. I know how to get around that. Get ready to jump on board, Sparrow.'

Twenty-one

Minou pressed her hands to her ears against the deafening clatter of the train. Smoke huffed from the funnel as it trundled closer, its brakes giving a long, eerie screech as it halted.

'Now, Sparrow!' Jay nudged her as passengers poured off and on to the track where the cows stood. The two of them threaded through the crowd, boarded the train and hurried along the empty compartments. They heard shouts and cheers as the cows were finally prodded off the track. Doors slammed up and down the carriages and the engine grumbled to life, ready to depart.

'First class? That's for Whitetowners – we're not allowed in here,' Minou whispered as they ducked into a compartment with plush upholstered seats.

Jay slammed the door behind them. 'We're not staying in first class – follow me.' He led her to the end of the train, opening the door and stepping on to the running board.

'I've done this journey without a ticket when money was short,' he explained. 'We can sit on the roof – I'll show you.'

Minou watched him scale a metal ladder to the roof, nimble as a monkey. She found it harder in her long dress – how much easier it would have been in her old tunic and trousers! Finally, she was up and flopped beside Jay. Smoke billowed from the funnel as the train moved off. Behind them, a deep orange sun sank over the dusty plain, ahead the foothills were silhouettes against the horizon. She couldn't help smirking at Jay, whose face was coated in grey soot, his windblown hair sticking up wildly.

'Something funny?'

'You look like a ghoul, risen from the grave!'

Jay gave a wry smile. 'No offence, Sparrow, but you don't look much better.'

The train slowed as it climbed the hills. They fell silent. Minou had never left Moonlally before, and she gazed around her curiously at the changing landscape, the dry land heaping into blue hills, the air turning cool and fragrant. Crickets chirruped in the undergrowth below the clamour of evening birdsong. From the rumbling roof, she watched her long shadow, wavering black over moving ground. Jay lay on his back, head on his hands and eyes closed. She could tell by his breathing that he wasn't asleep.

'Is this the train you took to school in Samudra?' she asked. 'Did you like it there?'

The boy opened his eyes. He shrugged. 'It was all right. I didn't want to leave Moonlally – but when Father died, I joined the rebels. Ma asked her brother in Samudra to take me in.' He squinted at the sky. 'She wanted me kept out of trouble.'

'What happened to your father?'

'He worked in the silver mines, south of Moonlally – conditions are deadly there. He complained to the bosses, but nothing changed. One day the roof caved in. Father went down to help rescue the other miners and—' Jay shrugged, wiping his dirty face with his sleeve – 'he never came out again.'

They were both silent. The train climbed on, huffing up the forested slopes with effort. Long crimson rays of sunset pierced the green canopy of trees.

'I'm so sorry, Jay. Your poor mother.' She glanced at his face, warmed by the light.

'Ma's been terrified of the General ever since. She wouldn't let Karu file a complaint. Too scared he'd disappear, like so many others have.'

'It's hard when you lose someone,' Minou said at last. 'You lose yourself as well. When Dima died, I felt I'd turned hard as a stone.' Like the fossil she'd found by the Lally. She'd shown it to Master Karu, who said it was once a living creature, hardened to rock over centuries. She shivered, remembering the terrible night she'd found Dima. 'The worst thing is, I don't understand why she had to die,' she told Jay, her voice choked. 'Who would kill Dima?' She wiped her tears away with her hand.

'Sparrow – are you all right?' Jay looked at her with concern.

'Dust, tickling my nose.' She sniffed. 'I didn't care when I was taken to the palace. I'd rather it was me than some other girl, one with a family to worry about her.'

'Sparrow— *Whoa!*' The train squealed to a shuddering halt, that almost had Jay sliding off the roof.

'What the—' Minou whispered, grabbing his jacket as he scrambled back up. 'Why have we stopped in the middle of the jungle?'

'Wild elephants, I reckon. There's a crossing here, trains often stop for them. We're not far from the next stop. A hill town called Karomsheel. The railway track changes to a narrow gauge there.'

'Wild *elephants!*' Minou peered down, hoping for a sight of them. A large yellow sign with a black elephant silhouette proclaimed:

ELEPHANT CROSSING.

PLEASE HALT HERE.

A loud trumpeting echoed through the forest. A herd was crossing the track ahead: three adult females nudging a reluctant infant. The passengers hung out of their windows, exclaiming at the sight.

'Jay – look, a baby elephant!' Minou whispered, scrambling closer to the edge of the roof. 'By the Lady, Ophelia would have loved this.'

'Careful now,' Jay warned. 'Wild elephants are dangerous.'

'But the baby's stuck! Poor thing's too scared to cross the tracks. The others have left it behind.'

She could see the herd moving off down the slope, their great feet thrashing loudly through the undergrowth. The frightened baby had scampered back and was sitting, trumpeting sadly, on the other side of the tracks.

'Jay, we can't leave a baby elephant. We have to help!' Minou slid over the edge of the roof and as silently as she could manage, made her way down the ladder.

'Sparrow, in the jungle you don't interfere with wildlife. And what if the other passengers see us?' Reluctantly, Jay swung himself after her. They crouched down to approach the baby elephant, seated in scrubby bushes by the railway line and sucking on its trunk.

'Sparrow, this is a bad idea—'

'We need to lure it over the tracks – look, figs!' Minou darted over to a scatter of windfallen fruit beneath a tree. 'The palace elephants love them.' She kneeled on the ground and stretched out her hand, holding a fig. The baby explored it with its trunk, harrumphing in surprise. 'Good elephant. Come on!' Minou said encouragingly, as it scrambled to its feet. She'd coaxed it halfway across the track when a blast of trumpeting carried over the trees.

'That's the mother coming back – run!' Jay called as he made for safety.

'*Wait!*' Minou called, trying to draw the baby further. The air split open with the fierce, full-blown sound of a large and furious mother elephant. Minou sprinted into the undergrowth, almost knocking Jay over.

'*Sparrow!* Thundering elephants – we could have been trampled to death!'

Minou beamed. 'But it worked. Look at the mother and baby, together again.'

The elephant herd had surrounded the baby and were nudging and fussing it gently over the crossing and down into the forest. Minou watched their great grey rumps swaying through the trees until they disappeared.

'They're gone,' she breathed.

The train whistle shrieked; the driver impatient to be on his way. The unexpected noise took the herd by surprise; the great creatures thrashed down the hillside. The train engine's chuff and rattle drowned out the thud of elephant feet as it moved off in a cloud of smoke.

'And... so is our train,' Jay added.

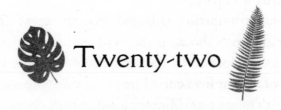

Twenty-two

Minou gave Jay an apologetic smile. 'There must be another train?'

The boy shook his head. 'Not today. And it's late. We can't stay here overnight.'

'What shall we do?'

Jay sighed. 'We could follow the railway line on to Karomsheel. If we spend the night there, we can take tomorrow's train.'

The tracks guided them deeper into lush forest. Huge rustling trees towered above, monkeys chattered and blue flycatchers and rose finches flitted between the green treetops.

'This place is beautiful!' Minou whispered.

'But dangerous,' Jay warned. 'There are leopards in this forest – maybe even tigers. Not to mention jackals and wild boar – the Whitetowners love hunting out here.'

The piercing sound of a bugle broke over the forest: three long calls followed by three short bursts.

'There, you see. That's the Commandant's bugle call,' Jay told her. 'He'll be on a night hunt – most likely after a leopard,'

A loud trumpeting volleyed around them. They could hear men's shouts as the elephant herd trampled through the forest. In the gathering darkness, the smoke of distant fires curled from the valley below.

'What's going on?' Minou pulled at Jay's sleeve.

'Sounds like the wild elephants we saw are headed for the hunting party. Hope they get trampled.'

The forest was ablaze with sound: the blast of elephants and a panicked banging of drums, followed by the crack and echo of gunfire. Birds flocked from the trees in alarm and a troop of monkeys just above them hooted and bared their teeth.

'We'd better climb a tree, in case they come this way,' Jay shouted.

Minou sized up a spreading sandalwood tree. With a leap, she grabbed a low branch and swung herself up halfway. From her vantage point, she could see a large fire burning in a clearing in the valley beneath them. Whitetowners in hunting clothes stood about, while bearers with flaming torches circled them in a ring,

'It is a hunt,' she called to Jay, a few branches below her. 'I can see torchbearers walking around the Whitetowners.'

'Trying to keep the wild elephants away.'

Minou shuffled forward on her branch for a better view. Far below, in the clearing's flickering light, she could see two big bamboo cages.

'Jay – it looks like they've got animals in cages.'

'Bait. A couple of goats to attract the leopard.'

The bugle call sounded once more and the Whitetowners mounted their vehicles, guided by their bearer's torches. Minou wondered if Tal and Little were among them. She saw the Whitetowners were riding mechanical elephants – far larger than those she'd seen in Shri's workshop.

'Moonlally's Marvellous Mechanicals!' she called. 'Jay, they've brought mechanical elephants to ride on for the hunt!'

Something thrashed in the undergrowth below. Minou held her breath, listening carefully to its jerky steps and urgent breathing. It wasn't a wild boar – she couldn't hear it snort or snuffle. Perhaps a deer? Curious, she slid down the tree trunk, so quickly that her dress ripped.

It was no animal, but a boy, alone and shivering. His clothes were streaked with mud, his face scratched and bleeding. And it was someone she knew – Tal, from Master Karu's school. She opened her mouth to speak but Tal put a finger to his lips. They listened as the bugle notes faded and the trampling crash of elephant feet died away. Jay dropped silently from the tree beside them. '*We have no hands, no face, no voice*,' he whispered.

'*Like the Lady, we thrive in darkness*,' the boy replied. 'It's you – the girl from school! And Master Karu's brother. What are you two doing out here?'

'Long story, Tal,' Jay said. 'Karu's been looking everywhere for you! Where's Little?'

The boy wiped his face with the hem of his shirt. 'What can I tell you? Police got us for that business with the statue. Took us in the same night – straight to the palace dungeons. Hey – you live in that old boat on the river, don't you?' he said, addressing Minou.

'I did, until my Dima died.' Minou muttered.

'The old lady died? I didn't know – I'm sorry. She tried to help us escape, you know. Took out a police car tyre with her pistol. By the Lady, the cops were furious!'

'Dima – are you sure?' Minou stammered.

'Yeah. We were running from the cathedral. She slowed them down, but they caught up with us.'

Minou swallowed. That explained the night of the gunshot. Dima had tried to save Tal and Little.

Jay glanced at her in sympathy. 'Why did they bring you out to the jungle, Tal?'

Tal groaned, his legs giving way as he slumped to the ground. 'Bait!' he gasped. 'They locked us in cages for the leopard hunt. When that herd of wild tuskers charged, I took my chance. Bashed the latch open and ran!'

'That's awful! Here–' Minou remembered the figs she'd knotted in her skirt while feeding the baby elephant 'squeeze the juice into your mouth.'

The boy did so, sucking the fruit and spitting out the skins as Minou watched him. She hadn't eaten all day and was hungry, but Tal looked half-starved. 'So it's true,' she whispered. 'The police handed you over to the General?'

The boy nodded, colour returning to his face. 'Mad as a rabid dog that one! He lent us to the Commandant for the hunt. Least we've got a chance of escaping out here – not like at the palace with the crocodiles.'

'And Little?' Minou asked. She'd wondered if Tal knew about the crocodiles in the moat.

'They've still got Little,' Tal told them, shaking his head. 'They'd have me, except a wild tusker took a dislike to the mechanicals and overturned one. It's tipped on the ground right there. Wish I knew how to drive the thing home.'

Jay shook his head. 'Don't go back to Moonlally. We've escaped the *Napoleon* and are on our way to Narsin. Come with us – you'll be safer.'

'Nah.' The boy wiped his sticky fingers on his shirt. 'Not leaving Little, am I. What kind of friend does that? I'll follow the hunt's tracks and spring him out.'

'You think you can?'

'I know I got to try. Reckon I'll sleep here, hitched to a tree branch. At dawn I'll follow their tracks home. Those mechanical elephants are like giant tractors – plough the ground up and demolish anything in their way.'

'If you're sure. Good luck, brother.' Jay shook his hand.

'May the Lady be with you,' Minou told him.

A grin broke over Tal's face. 'And with you! The Commandant said two fugitives escaped the airship. You'd better stay out of his way!' With that, he slunk off, fading into the forest as quickly as he'd appeared.

Twenty-three

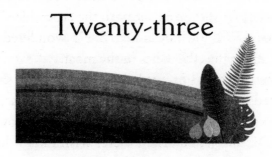

They picked their way along the railway line in the dusk. Minou wanted to look at the clearing below, to see the mechanical elephant abandoned by the Whitetowners, but Jay insisted they keep moving. 'Thundering elephants, Sparrow! We don't want to end up in the jungle all night – it's already black as the grave. Besides, the Whitetowners are bound to come back for their precious mechanical. They know we've escaped the airship. The last thing we need is a run-in with the Commandant.'

Minou sighed. Jay was right. But Shri had shown her how the elephant worked, and she couldn't help thinking how much fun it would be to swipe it from under the Commandant's nose.

Above, on the hillside, the Samudra train wheezed smoke, its twin yellow lamps illuminating the forest, as it ploughed to the summit and the hill town of Karomsheel.

Minou broke the silence. 'We're nearly as fast as the train on this slope.'

'Sparrow, listen.'

'What?'

'No more rescue missions. We're here to find the Queen – not save baby animals.'

'But—' Minou began. If they hadn't helped the baby elephant, the herd wouldn't have stampeded. And if the herd hadn't stampeded, how would Tal have escaped the hunting party?

'Sparrow, this is important. You're a Green Orchid now. We have to be disciplined.'

Minou frowned, annoyed. This was her idea in the first place – had Jay forgotten? He was only here because of her! But then, she was only here because of him. If she hadn't met Jay, she'd never have joined the Green Orchids. She decided to hold her tongue.

They walked on, the long grass rustling with night creatures and owls hooting, long and low overhead.

'What was that about crocodiles?' Jay asked her.

Minou shivered. 'The General throws prisoners to the crocodiles in his moat. It's true – I heard it from Ophelia herself.'

'By the Lady!' Jay spat on the ground. 'He's mad as a rabid dog all right. I hope Tal manages to catch up with Little in time.'

'Before, when I first met you, I didn't know much about the Green Orchids. Dima never told me she was one of the rebels.'

'She wanted to protect you. So, what do you think of us now?'

Minou's hands curled into fists as she remembered

Tal's scratched face and panicked footsteps. Like a frightened animal. How many children had been taken to the General's fortress, thrown to the crocodiles and never seen again? Dima had tried to save the two boys. Perhaps she'd even been killed for it.

'I'm proud to be a Green Orchid now,' she told him. 'We must find the Queen and overthrow the General. I want a tattoo and everything.'

'A tattoo like this one?' Jay hitched up the ripped sleeve of his jacket. A tiny emblem of three petals was inked on to his left shoulder. 'What if we get captured, like Tal and Little?'

Minou shrugged. 'Dima's dead and there isn't anyone else. I don't care about the danger – I want to help.'

Jay smiled, his teeth white in the darkness. 'Sparrow, you said that on the train. It's not true that you don't have anyone. You have us – we're family now. Me and the other Green Orchids.'

'So can I? Get a tattoo?'

Jay laughed. 'Being loyal to the cause counts for more than a tattoo.'

They hiked along the track, over cuttings and through tunnels hollowed from grey mountain rock. The lights of Karomsheel drew closer. When they came to a weathered wooden gate, Minou sniffed.

'Woodsmoke! Jay – let's take a look in here.'

'Why? Wait, Sparrow!'

But Minou had already hopped over the rickety gate and darted up the path. It led to a graveyard,

167

smaller than Blacktown's, and abandoned. By the look of the overgrown paths and neglected tombs, no funeral had taken place here for some time. She saw a faint orange glow in one corner. A fire, smouldering in a stone urn, smoke drifting down the hillside. The old cemetery wasn't deserted – someone lived here. And who would make their home in a graveyard but—

'Farisht?' Jay had followed her up the path. 'By the *Lady*!'

'And her thundering elephants!' A familiar face grinned at them from the shadows, his gold earring glinting. 'Jay and Miss Rosa's foundling – what was your name?'

'Call me Sparrow – everyone else does.'

Farisht waved his hand with a flourish. 'Well, Jay and Sparrow, I know this place doesn't look like much but it's ours for now. I'm glad you two birds flew up and found me. The rebel network must be better than I thought.'

They huddled around the fire and Farisht took out a bag of spiced peanuts and puffed rice for them to share. 'Blacktown street food!' Minou said happily. 'Farisht, you won't believe how long it is since I tasted this.' She told Farisht of her adventures and he shook his head in wonder.

'What an amazing story! So, the Batkeeper is the General's daughter?'

'Yes – she's an admirer of your poems. The bats carry them to her, like messages. That's how she became a Green Orchid.'

'All poems are messages, Sparrow – the best of them fly straight to the heart. But how did Ophelia discover that the Queen was alive in the first place?'

'Ophelia heard the General and Commandant talking. And then Shri, the palace clockmaker, told her that when the young queen fled the palace, he made her wax effigy to be buried at the funeral,' Minou told him. 'He also remembered that the Queen wrote letters to a friend while held captive. Ophelia found the map among them.'

'May I take a look?'

Minou fished the map out of her boot and the three of them pored over it by the dying light of the fire.

Farisht whistled. 'You're telling me that the Queen of Moonlally is alive and barely two days' journey away? Now this – *this* is poetry. But we'll need to make haste. It's not long until the monsoon reaches the hills and descends towards Moonlally. Every thirteen years the Lady's powers rise – this is the right time for the Queen's return.'

'When did you leave Moonlally, Farisht?' Jay broke in. 'I went to look for you at the cemetery, but you'd gone.'

Farisht nodded. 'I left the day after the funeral, I got word that there was a warrant out for my arrest. My funeral song for the General was a little too popular. I decided to make myself scarce. I've been roughed up by the police before, but Luna's too fragile for that kind of treatment.'

'Who's Luna?'

'Haven't you met Luna? Come, this way.' Farisht lit a candle stub in the fire and beckoned Minou across the graveyard. Concealed behind the largest tomb was a battered leather case with worn straps, the size of a large travelling trunk. Farisht unlocked it carefully. By the flicker of candlelight, Minou saw a polished wooden box with the brassy gleam of three lenses projecting from it.

'Is it a camera?'

'No, no – cameras are too expensive for someone like me. Luna here is my old magic lantern.' Farisht patted the wooden box lovingly. 'All we need is a black cloth, a flash of limelight and we'll put on a show fit for a queen! We've played the finest mansions in Whitetown.'

'I remember the lantern show at Dima's funeral – it was magical.'

Farisht grinned. 'That was no magic, but a special art, Sparrow! Luna and I tell tales of this world and the next with our pictures. We know all the stories of Moonlally.'

'You could tell our story, Farisht,' Minou suggested. 'Our death-defying leap from the General's airship. By the Lady, people would pay to see that!'

Farisht smiled. 'That's a good idea. It's wonderful to see Moonlally faces again. I've been lonely with only the ghost to talk to.'

'Ghost?' Minou raised an eyebrow. 'You've seen a ghost?' It was hard to tell when Farisht was joking.

He nodded. 'Cemeteries are full of them. This one's abandoned, but there's one ghost left. An old man who came to Indica to study plants, hundreds of years ago. This is his tomb.'

'But why does he haunt the graveyard?' Minou asked, looking warily around her. If ghosts were real, this abandoned cemetery was exactly the sort of place they might linger.

Farisht glanced about and leaned closer, lowering his voice. 'It's a long story. He was born into a different religion. After he converted, the authorities accused him of practising his in secret and executed him. Old Gaston wanders the cemetery, searching for wild herbs… frankly, he's a bit of a bore about them.'

'Gaston d'Aragord? You don't mean the doctor who wrote the *Botanica of Southern Indica*?'

'The same.'

'Poor Gaston.' Minou felt a wave of sadness for the doctor's ghost. 'Mamzelle made me copy watercolours from his book in the palace. But he must love it here – look at the wild garlic, spikenard and mint – all sorts of remedies!' She glanced up at Farisht. 'I've seen a ghost too – kind of.'

'How so?'

'You know they say the Dark Lady's spirit haunts the palace? Well, I think I saw her.'

'Tell me more?'

'She was a shadowy woman in black robes. It was hard to see her face, but her eyes burned bright – like coals in a fire. Do you think I imagined it? Dima saw her, but I never did before. I didn't tell Mamzelle – she wouldn't have believed me.'

Farisht nodded thoughtfully. 'They say the Lady's spirit walks the palace, ever since the General seized power. You know the hymn, of course? The song of the Dark Lady.'

'Dima sang it every morning. But I never learned it properly,' Minou admitted.

'I'll teach you,' Farisht told her, patting Minou on the shoulder. 'The Dark Lady doesn't appear to everyone. If you respect her, she'll help you. But you're shivering. We'd better get back to the fire. Shall we hide the map in Luna's case? It'll be safer there.'

Minou agreed and they slid the map carefully between Luna's leather case and her wooden exterior. They returned to the smouldering fire to find Jay stretched out on the ground, fast asleep and snoring. Settling beside him, Minou closed her eyes. Despite the hard ground, she fell asleep instantly. All night, she dreamed restlessly of her leap from the *Napoleon* into the sea, the sound of the wind through the trees becoming waves, crashing over a sandy shore.

Twenty-four

Minou opened her eyes to find the graveyard shrouded in mist. They were so high up, clouds obscured half the hillside. At the far summit, she could make out a faint huddle of colourful buildings, floating above the white haze. That must be the hill town of Karomsheel.

She hugged herself against the chill of dawn as Jay, wrapped in an old blanket, slept on. Farisht woke and greeted her, lighting the fire to brew chai. He handed her a steaming cup and they watched the clouds ebb away and the mist begin to clear. Green slopes reappeared around them, terraced with fields and orchards. A chorus of birdsong soared as the sun rose crimson, scattering the mist into a shimmering rainbow. Minou thought it was the most beautiful place she'd ever seen.

'Farisht,' she said, remembering. 'What did you mean about the Lady's powers growing stronger every thirteen years? Dima said something similar – that the river would rise soon. She was worried about floods – the land's been dry for so long.'

'Do you remember the huge storm, thirteen years ago?' Farisht frowned. 'No, you're too young. I was only a small boy at the time, five or six.'

Minou clapped her hands. 'That was the night I was found! In a boat washed up on the riverbank. By Father Jacob, the Whitetown priest.'

'You mean you're a foundling like me, Sparrow? Many strange things happened that night. I remember, two women sheltered in our graveyard. The younger one had hurt her ankle and had to lean on her old companion. My father let them stay until she recovered. But didn't I say I'd teach you the hymn to the Lady? That tells the prophecy better than I can.'

Minou nodded, eager to hear Farisht sing. He cleared his throat and began in his clear, low voice:

'Dark Lady, born of the clouded hills,
whose songs summon the rains down still,
whose third eye spears as lightning strike,
whose powers turn back the highest tide.
Your radiance rivals the silver moon,
your anger brings tempest with monsoon.
Grant us blessings in pearls from oceans deep.
May your amber gaze heal those that weep.
Beloved of poets, weavers of words,
your soft voice tames wild elephant herds.
When the floodwaters rise at year thirteen,
to renew red earth and clothe her green,
then anoint our queendom's rightful queen.

Minou repeated the words after him until she had them memorised. She touched the tin elephant, nestling warm at her throat. 'Farisht – I promise I'll try and sing it every morning, like Dima used to. But I didn't know you were a foundling too?'

'I am indeed.' He smiled at her.

'Do you know anything about your parents?'

'Only that my mother was from Blacktown and in service to a rich Whitetown family. She couldn't keep me, so she gave me to the graveyard poet to raise. He became my adopted father. My mother died soon afterwards.'

Minou thought over Farisht's words. 'But why couldn't she keep you?'

'Sparrow, the world is a complicated place and Moonlally especially so. You look a bit like me, a mixture of Whitetown and Blacktown. Blacktowners and Whitetowners aren't allowed to marry, you know. Except for the General – who plasters his face in white paint and pretends he's a Whitetowner.'

Minou examined the light brown of her arms. Could it be true she was part Whitetowner? A few days in the General's palace had turned her skin slightly paler. She'd put Farisht's own pallor down to living among the graves. She turned to look at Jay, whose skin was a deep, burnished mahogany like other Blacktowners, his hair black and shiny as a raven's wing.

At that moment the boy yawned, stretched and reached gratefully for his tea. 'By the Lady! It's cold as the grave in these hills,' he shivered. 'Are we off? We must catch the next train to Narsin. For all we know, the *Napoleon*'s crew have set the Moonlally police on us. We need to keep moving.'

'And they'd love to get their hands on me. I'd better buy us new clothes, so we're dressed like the hill people,' Farisht told them. 'It wouldn't hurt you both to wash – there's a stream close by. You look like you've been dragged through the jungle by wild elephants! What colour would you like, Sparrow?'

'Colour?' Minou mused over the question. The tunic and trousers she'd worn with Dima were so faded, they'd barely had a colour. Since then, she had dressed in white muslin or lace. She tilted her face up to the sky. The sun had burned off the mist to a perfect blue. 'I'd like blue, please, Farisht.'

They found the stream and washed in the icy water, among tiny silvery fish. Farisht returned with goat's cheese pancakes, warm from the griddle, and their new clothes. Minou ripped the parcel open to find a blue skirt embroidered with red flowers, a blue tunic and a padded red waistcoat. She spun on the spot, the skirt twirling around her. 'Is this what they wear in the hills? Farisht, it's lovely – thank you!'

'We don't want to attract attention,' Jay grumbled, fastening his indigo kilt. 'Rub in some dirt, so they don't look new.'

'Now what?' Minou exclaimed, scooping handfuls of graveyard dirt and rubbing it into her clothes. 'Let's go into Karomsheel!'

'Yes – but please be careful,' Farisht told them. 'I'll buy our train tickets to Narsin. Keep your guard up.'

They climbed the hill, listening to Farisht sing, his deep voice carrying on the cool breeze:

'Two crocodiles lurk
In a stone-hearted city.
With yellow eyes
And reptilian stares
They wait to snare
All those who dare
Defy their evil work.'

'The Commandant and the General – what a pair of villains,' Farisht sighed. 'But where there's life there's hope and where there's hope, everything can begin again. Even Moonlally.'

Minou gazed about her as they approached Karomsheel. The market square was large and well kept, fruit boxes brimmed with purple figs, cherries and plums. Aromas of spit-grilled chicken, smoked tea and rosewater drifted from the food stalls. 'Colours!' she exclaimed, pointing out a stall heaped with powdered dyes: vermillion red, gold ochre, indigo and lapis blue. 'What are they for?'

'Dyeing clothes, I expect.' Farisht nodded at the railway station. 'I'm going in here. You two wait outside while I buy our tickets.'

Minou settled on the station steps, smiling at the curious stares of passers-by. Karomsheel was such a small town that strangers drew attention, however they were dressed. Girls in bright skirts edged with tiny bells jingled past, carrying garlands of flowers to a building on the far side of the square.

'I'm off to look in there, Jay.'

'The temple? All right, but don't go adopting any stray wildcats.'

Minou followed the swaying walk of the hill girls. Gathering a handful of fallen flowers from the steps, she watched as they rang a bell and entered. She peeked into the doorway – she'd never been inside a temple, except the one in Shri's warehouse, for they no longer existed in Moonlally.

She sniffed at the scent of incense, familiar to her from Dima's altar. Along the far wall, alcoves each held a different icon of the old gods. A god with matted locks, like Nala the holy man, danced in a ring of flames. A beautiful goddess rode upon a swan. She recognised the elephant-headed god from Karu's stories.

But when she tugged the bell to enter, a woman at the doorway swished a curtain over the entrance, blocking her view. 'The temple is closing now, child. There's trouble in the marketplace.'

Reluctantly, Minou turned back to the square, shading her eyes against the bright sunlight as she searched for Jay. The low buzz of the market had fallen silent. He wasn't on the steps where she'd left him and a crowd had gathered in the centre.

What was going on?

In a panic, she pushed through to see Farisht, flanked by two Moonlally policemen. As she watched, one grabbed his canvas knapsack and flung its contents to the floor, the other stamping on it. Minou winced at the sickening crunch of broken glass, thankful the map and Farisht's magic lantern were safe in the old cemetery.

'*Sparrow!*' Jay hissed at her from a fruit stall. 'Over here!' She darted towards him and dived behind a display of oranges.

'What do we do, Jay?'

Jay shook his head. 'Nothing we can do. They're armed, Sparrow.'

'But we've got to do *something*.' Desperately, she watched the men strutting around Farisht. One jabbed a bony finger into Farisht's face. Jay was right – she could see a pistol in the holster at his belt.

Minou picked up a bruised orange from the ground and weighed it in her hand. Perhaps she could distract the police. As one turned, she lobbed the overripe fruit and ducked. It hit him squarely in the middle of his back, exploding in a mess of juice over his khaki uniform.

'Who did that?' Scowling with fury, the policeman stalked towards the unsuspecting fruit-stall owner. 'How dare you?' To Minou's horror, he raised his truncheon to strike him. But his hand was gripped firmly by a stocky man, dressed in the blue kilt of the hills. The policeman struggled to pull free.

'How dare you lay a hand on me? Who do you think you are?'

'I'm the Mayor of Karomsheel, since you ask,' the hefty man replied, puffing out his broad chest and cracking his knuckles. 'I'm in charge here. You can't go round arresting people in my town! What's this young lad done?'

'He's a traitor! I'm Moonlally's chief of police and I have a warrant for his arrest.'

'On what charge?'

'He broke the law prohibiting performances of a defamatory nature.'

The mayor shrugged, miming confusion.

'He insulted the General! With – a popular song—' the policeman spluttered.

The mayor laughed, other locals joining in. '*Ooh!* He insulted the General, did he? You mean that pasty-faced, moustachioed madman in his hot-air balloon? Whoops – you'd better arrest me too!' He stepped closer to the policemen, huge fists raised in front of his barrel chest.

A crowd gathered behind him, the fruit-stall owner with them, holding up a giant eggplant. 'Arrest me too!' he yelled. They all laughed and cries swept across the marketplace.

'Take us all in!'

'Everyone knows the General's cracked in the head!'

'Let him go!' the police chief fumed. At his word, the other men released Farisht. 'You won't get away with this, I warn you,' he barked at the mayor. 'These towns are lawless – I'll bet other fugitives hide out here – like those kids that jumped from the *Napoleon*. The Commandant's on his way to the hills to find them.'

'You bring the Commandant to see me! I've got a thing or two to say to him,' the mayor told him. 'He's tried to close down our temples. Built railways through our fields. Now he expects us to pay taxes? Ridiculous!'

The townspeople gathered around Farisht. Minou watched the policemen leave the marketplace, slowly brandishing their truncheons. Once they were out of sight, she made her way to the front of the crowd, Jay by her side.

'Farisht – are you all right? Your beautiful glass slides…'

He smiled at her. 'I'm fine, Sparrow, thanks to the mayor. And I can paint more.'

The mayor's name was Malkan, and he insisted they eat lunch at his stall. 'Don't insult me!' he growled when they tried to pay for the grilled chicken and flatbread. 'I'm in charge. And who are you two kids? Has all Moonlally come to the hills?'

Minou and Jay told him of their adventures as they ate, the big man's eyes almost popping out of his head. 'What a story! I'd like you to tell it to the whole town!'

'Let's do that tonight,' Farisht suggested. 'We'll give the town a magic lantern performance, to show our thanks before travelling on.'

'But we must get to Narsin!' Minou broke in. 'The monsoon's coming. Farisht – you said now was the time…' She tailed off, not knowing how much of their quest to share with Malkan.

'And the police know we've escaped the airship,' Jay added. 'Didn't they say the Commandant's on his way? Sparrow's right, we need to move on.'

'The police are watching the train station. Let me think.' Malkan scratched his chin. 'I know an overland route to the temple – but it's dangerous! There are bandits in these hills.'

'We're not scared of bandits,' Minou put in. 'Jay and I are kalari fighters. We could have thrashed those policemen – even with their guns!'

Malkan thumped his great chest and laughed until tears streamed from his eyes. 'A kitten who thinks she's a tiger. I've never heard anything so funny! If you were old enough, I'd marry you to my eldest son. He has his own goats, you know. Six of them!'

Minou scowled and was about to put him straight but caught Farisht's warning glance. She settled for shooting Malkan a look that would have melted butter.

'Wonderful! We're agreed, then,' Farisht interrupted hastily. 'A magic lantern show – at midnight in the square. And first thing tomorrow, we'll travel over the hills to the temple at Narsin. Malkan, could you ask someone to watch the police? I don't want to start the show until they've moved on. We'll lay low in the graveyard until nightfall.'

'The old graveyard? So that's where you've been hiding out! Don't worry, I'll get my eldest – the goatherd – to keep lookout.'

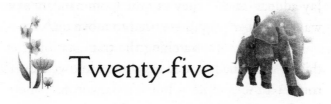

Twenty-five

Night fell swiftly in the hills. The hooting of owls and a faint trumpeting of elephants carried from the valley below. They were preparing for their performance amid the graveyard's tumbledown tombs. Minou fanned a new set of magic lantern slides dry, painted to replace those the policemen smashed. Farisht scribbled notes by the flicker of a candle, while Jay had gone to find Malkan's son, for news of the Moonlally police.

A clamour of tinkling bells signalled Jay's return with the goatherd and his flock. Minou ran to the cemetery gate to pet the small white goats and was welcomed by a chorus of bleats.

'Come in! Bring your goats with you – the grass in here's overgrown!' Farisht called. The boy shook his head shyly.

'He won't set foot in the graveyard. Scared of ghosts,' Jay explained.

'I'm not scared!' the boy protested. 'But if our goats eat the grass that grows over the dead, we believe their milk will turn sour.'

'What's with the policemen?' Minou asked.

Jay grimaced. 'They're still at the railway station. They've asked our friend here to bring them goat's milk – shame we can't turn that sour.'

Farisht sighed. 'I think we'll cancel our show. Too risky with the police.'

Minou sprang to her feet, remembering the potion she'd memorised from d'Aragord's *Botanica*. 'By the Lady! We won't need to cancel the show if they're fast asleep. Look – there are spikenard plants in this cemetery. You crush the root and boil it with milk – it's a powerful sleeping draught.'

An hour later, she'd dug out six fat roots, washed and ground them into a paste. 'Here,' she said, handing it to Malkan's son. 'Mix a teaspoon of *this* into their milk!'

The young goatherd looked worried. 'You sure it won't poison them?'

Minou shook her head. 'Not a bit! Mamzelle uses it all the time – it isn't dangerous. They'll sleep like the dead, then wake up with a headache.'

Malkan's son shrugged. 'I'll try it. Tell you what, if it works, I'll signal at the cemetery gate. Three whistles mean it's safe.'

Later that night, when they heard the goatherd's three long whistles, they were ready. Luna, the magic lantern, was packed safely in her case and strapped on to Farisht's back, Minou hauled a roll of black cloth to make a tent for the show and Jay carried a bunch of young tree saplings to use as tent poles.

'The policemen are snoring away,' the boy told them, as they made their way up the hill in the wake of his lamp. 'Dunno if it was the stuff I added to the milk or the stationmaster's rum!'

The town square appeared deserted but as they staked the tent poles, Malkan and others appeared from the shadows to help. A makeshift tent was assembled against the white temple wall, turning it into a blank screen for Luna to project her magic lantern images. All the townspeople, even babies, were packed inside. Farisht struck a match. With a hiss and spark of flame and a flare of limelight, a painting of the General's face appeared on the wall, to jeers and boos. Karomsheel's people settled in for the night's entertainment.

'Once there was a demon king with... not one. Not two! But *three heads*!' Farisht used Luna's three lenses to triple the moustachioed head of the General and was rewarded by shrieks and gasps. 'Many heroes tried to save the people from his tyranny...'

Two of the General's heads were swiped away, leaving one scowling on the temple wall. The crowd cheered. 'But – the demon king was invincible! Until the day two young people blessed with the power of flight boarded his sky palace.'

Minou handed Farisht the next slide and a painted image of the *Napoleon* glowed purple on the temple wall, two bat-winged figures suspended below the airship's gondola.

'They tried to defeat the demon king, to no avail! For his heads regrew each time he was slain. So, they made for the hills.' Farisht moved the glass panels in and out, showing the winged figures swooping over blue-painted slopes.

'In the hills, they prayed to the goddess to help them defeat the demon king. The goddess flew to his lair, and with a single glance from her third eye, turned him to a heap of ashes!'

A painting of the General's head appeared, surrounded by orange flames. The crowd roared approval. Farisht ended the show with his funeral song for the General. A flask of rum was passed around and the people of Karomsheel clapped and stamped their feet to the beat. It reminded Minou of her first meeting of the Green Orchids, the night of Dima's funeral. How little she'd known then of what was to come.

'Why did you change our story, Farisht?' Minou asked as they followed the moonlit path down to the cemetery. 'You know – the way you turned the General into a demon king and us into bat-winged heroes.'

'Stories work best that way, I've found, Sparrow. You give people a golden thread of truth, hidden within a colourful weave of magic. Let them unravel it for themselves. Do you understand?'

'Not really,' Minou mused. 'Maybe I haven't heard enough stories. Dima only told them on Sundays – mostly about the old days.'

Farisht laughed. 'Stories matter. A land that loses its stories loses its way. They're lights, guiding us along the path ahead. Perhaps that's what happened to Moonlally.'

Minou was too excited to sleep that night. Farisht's words made her think. Had she really seen the Dark Lady in the palace? If she'd asked Dima, her grandmother would have said *yes*. But Mamzelle, with her natural philosophy, would state firmly that Minou had imagined it – the Dark Lady was only a creation of her mind.

Could belief in magic make the unimaginable real? Perhaps Farisht's lantern shows were not just entertainment. Perhaps seeing herself and Jay vanquish the General – with the Dark Lady's help – was what made his defeat possible.

The following morning, Farisht woke them early to trek to the temple overland. 'I know it's a longer journey, but it's dangerous to go by train if the Commandant's on his way. We'll have to leave Luna behind. She's too heavy to carry over the hills. Which is a shame because we need money. I'm almost down to my last pagoda.'

'But wait – what if we could carry Luna?' Minou leaped to her feet with excitement.

'How, Sparrow? Do you have a spare pony and cart?'

'No, but I know where there's something better – a mechanical elephant!'

Jay groaned. 'Not that elephant again.'

After Minou had explained to Farisht, he decided it was worth a look. They left Luna in the graveyard and followed the railway down the hillside. Malkan and his friends came too, carrying stout ropes and wooden planks.

'I'm telling you, that mechanical's long gone,' Jay muttered. 'Those Whitetowners will have hauled it home.'

But the great elephant lay there still, tipped on its side in the clearing, its wood darkened by damp and scattered with leaves. A squirrel scuttled out of its belly as they approached. Other than charred torches lying on the ground, there was no sign of the Whitetowners.

'Look at this beast!' Malkan bellowed. 'Why, it could plough my fields better than six buffalo!'

The men of Karomsheel circled the elephant in appreciation, banging its flanks and admiring the wide rubber tracks, which allowed it to roll over uneven ground like a tractor. They hauled ropes around its belly and pushed planks under its back, resting them on a fallen log. Some heaved, others acted as counterweights, until they had levered the huge wooden elephant upright.

'What a marvellous invention!' Farisht shook his head in amazement. 'And there's a water tank connected to its trunk. Shri's a genius. Who would think of fitting Universal Railway Tracks on to a carved mahogany elephant with brass trimmings?'

'And an internal two-stroke engine, more to the point.' Jay had poked around inside the elephant's belly as it lay on its side. 'What good will it be once it runs out of fuel?'

'There's optional manpower – look!' Minou swung open the door to the driver's compartment. As Shri had shown her, there were two sets of cycle pedals that allowed the elephant to be driven manually.

'Tough work, pedalling up those hills,' Jay objected.

'But if we save fuel for inclines and use manpower for the flat, it might work!' Farisht exclaimed. 'Let's drive it to the cemetery and tie Luna onto its back.'

Hours later, Minou sat upon a mechanical wooden elephant, resting against Luna's leather case. Jay and Farisht were inside the elephant, pedalling. The sun had sunk below the horizon, a bone-coloured moon gleamed in the indigo sky. The mechanical's tracks rumbled loudly over the pebbled surface of the sloping path, but the ride was surprisingly smooth. Karomsheel was behind them now. The railway was a black scar, tunnelling through the hills below, while the road ahead twisted through terraced fields and craggy slopes.

Malkan had supplied them with dried goat's meat, apples and plums from his orchard and fresh water to fill the tank in the elephant's head. 'Good luck! But take care, there are bandits in these hills,' he warned. 'Narsin's only days away on that marvellous elephant. You can't miss the temple, it's huge. And you'll see the pilgrims on their way to the festival.'

They stopped at the next village, a mere scattering of huts, but the villagers were friendly. They exclaimed at the wondrous elephant and were entranced by Farisht's magic lantern show. To his delight, they offered free food and lodging for the night in return for entertainment.

'At this rate, we won't need any money!' Farisht told them. 'Once people see our marvellous mechanical, they can't do enough for us. If we weren't in search of the Queen, I'd deck her in silks and tassels and go to Samudra to make our fortune! Samudra's streets are packed with jugglers, acrobats and musicians, but they'll never have seen anything like her. We should give her a name. How about Laxmi – goddess of wealth?'

'Laxmi! That's perfect. I'd like to visit Samudra,' Minou told him. 'We could go after we've found the Queen. Jay and I could do acrobatics–'

Jay cleared his throat. 'I think you're both forgetting we took Laxmi from the Commandant's hunting party. I'm not sure we want all the attention she's attracting.'

Minou nodded. She glanced behind her, uneasy at the muddy tracks Laxmi had made. Were the Moonlally policemen following them?

The three travellers quickly fell into a rhythm. They woke, washed and took it in turns to pilot Laxmi up slopes and around twisting bends. Her inner compartment was a wonder, fitted with seats for those pedalling and a steering wheel. A window between her front legs allowed the drivers to see out, though whoever rode on top needed to keep watch. Luckily, they didn't come across another vehicle on their journey.

When darkness fell, they stopped at hamlets so small that they had no name. The hill folk welcomed the sight of the elephant, trundling over the rough terrain. She might lack silks and tassels, but her brass was polished to a shine and they kept her tracks free of stones.

At each stop, children queued for rides on Laxmi, while Farisht delighted the people with magic-lantern tales of the old gods. Minou learned how the elephant-headed god broke off his own tusk to use as a pen, and how the monkey god, son of the wind, crossed an ocean to rescue a princess. She noted that Farisht didn't tell of Minou and Jay's winged escape from the demon king's sky ship again. Perhaps he was worried that the Moonlally police were on their trail? She knew Jay was – she'd noticed him trying to brush away Laxmi's tracks whenever they left a settlement.

But the journey to Narsin continued smoothly and Minou tried to push these thoughts from her mind. Although they were warned again of bandits, they met with no danger on their travels, other than snakes slithering across stony paths and once a black panther, standing proud on a steep ravine.

On their third night of travelling, the head of a village they'd stopped at seemed less friendly. He urged them onwards, dismissing Farisht's offer of a magic lantern show. 'Don't stop here – you're almost at Narsin!' he told them. 'The temple's just over the next summit. You'd be better off camping at the top – there's a spring there. Then it's downhill all the way.'

The three of them reached the spring long after nightfall, too tired to go further and collapsed on to the hard ground without any supper. Minou yawned. 'What a shame we didn't get to hear your stories of the old gods tonight, Farisht. Why don't people tell them in Moonlally?'

'They did in the time of the old queen. She held festivals with musicians and storytellers. But when the General seized power, they stopped. People forgot the old gods.'

'Though not the Dark Lady. People still remember her. Shri's hidden her icon behind his warehouse, in a secret temple.'

'You mean the famous icon – the one with a black diamond as her third eye?'

'Except her third eye's gone. It disappeared when the young queen fled.'

'Well, little wonder her spirit haunts the palace. The third eye is the source of her power. Without it, she can't protect the city. Do you know the story of how the first Queen of Moonlally became the Dark Lady?'

They both did, but listened gladly anyway, as Farisht told it so well.

In days of old, a beautiful queen ruled Moonlally. Having no wish to marry, the royal priest told her to pray to the gods for a child – in this way, her successor would be divine.

The Queen left the royal palace, took off her silks and jewels and dressed in the coarsest cloth. Sheltering in the hills, she gathered nuts and berries to live on and prayed by day and night. After thirteen years, the gods, pleased by her penance, granted her a beautiful baby girl.

In her absence, an enemy king invaded Moonlally. The Queen had an heir, but no queendom. She rode home from the hills, her daughter tied to her back. On entering the city, she was dragged from her horse by enemy soldiers.

The gods were enraged by this insult. The sky turned black, stars fell, one by one, shooting through the skies. The Queen approached the palace gates to confront her enemy. A fallen star landed in the centre of her forehead and stayed, glittering, as her magical third eye.

The enemy king cowered, begging forgiveness, as the Queen unleashed a bolt of lightning from her third eye, reducing him to a smouldering heap of ashes.

The gods cried heavenly tears of joy at the rightful queen's return, flooding the land with their divine blessings. And that is why, every thirteen years, the rains cause the Lally to flood, and the Queen and her heir seek the Dark Lady's protection once more.

Twenty-six

They woke to a rose-coloured dawn and found themselves at the summit of a steep hill. Green slopes descended to a vast plateau where a monumental temple stood, its tiered steps carved from pink marble and bathed in pale light. They'd reached Narsin at last.

'What's happening down there?' Minou pointed to a costumed procession, snaking towards the temple.

'Those are pilgrims, here for the festival,' Farisht explained. 'Narsin's such an important temple, even the Whitetowners dare not close it down. People come from all over Indica.'

Minou stared entranced at the many-armed cavalcade of gods and goddesses – masked and painted people – riding in carts shaped like lotus flowers or swans. She recognised them from Farisht's show: the monkey warrior, the blue-skinned dancer rattling his drum, and her favourite, the elephant-headed scribe. Behind them, a troupe of yellow-clad dancers held flaming torches, smoke drifting high into the mountain air. Following them were drummers, their thudding beat carrying faintly up the hillside. Bringing up the rear of the procession were elephants, as gorgeously dressed as the people.

'I'm starving,' Jay grunted. 'Let's hope the food's free at this festival. Even with Laxmi, we've got competition when it comes to entertainment.'

Farisht laughed. 'True! Why don't we leave Luna and Laxmi up here and visit the temple? We should seek the old gods' blessings before we go on to find the Queen. According to the map, we're not far from the nuns' village now.'

Halfway down the slope, a thicket of scrubby trees sprang from the hillside. They helped Farisht to steer Laxmi into it, hiding Luna in her belly and covered the wooden elephant with branches and grass. Minou's stomach growled so loudly they all heard it.

'Right. Time for temple food! Sweetmeats and spicy beans, coconut rice and mangoes…' Farisht announced. 'Laxmi's hidden – if it's possible to hide a three-metre mechanical elephant.' He marked the clump of trees with a scrap of cloth, torn from his yellow shirt.

They ventured down to the plateau as the procession of pilgrims disappeared inside the gates. The temple complex was laid out like a village, with small buildings arranged around the large inner shrine. Incense smoke veiled the air, the place thronged with pilgrims, buying garlands of golden marigolds and fragrant jasmine to offer the gods. Children ran about, calling and shrieking over the murmuring chant of priests. Everywhere, tales of the gods were being sung or recited.

Farisht stopped by a group reading from a huge book. 'I've never heard this epic! It takes the priests seven days and nights to recite the whole story. I must listen for a while.'

'But we're starving!' Jay groaned. 'Food…'

'Why don't you two go and eat? I'll catch up with you. Then we'll pay our respects at the Dark Lady's altar – together.'

Jay and Minou followed the crowd to the temple gardens, where a large white tent had been pitched. Pilgrims lined up for a banana-leaf plate of rice, beans and mango pickle. They joined them, carrying their laden plates beyond the crowded gardens and on to a pebbled road leading higher into the hills. They climbed the bank and scrambled on to a flat boulder. Distant jangling music carried from the temple, but otherwise all was peaceful. After they'd eaten, Jay flopped down in the warm sun and yawned.

'Jay – you can't go to sleep. Let's explore.'

'Five minutes,' Jay murmured, closing his eyes.

Minou hugged her knees. The afternoon sun was warm on her back and a cool breeze stirred the air. Soon, with the Dark Lady's blessing, they'd find the Queen and complete their mission. Then came the important part, to spread news of the Queen's return and encourage the people of Blacktown to overthrow the General. She wanted the General gone. But secretly, she wished the three of them could keep travelling for ever. She loved the freedom of the road, riding on Laxmi and giving magic lantern shows with Farisht and Luna. Now Dima was gone, what was left for her in Moonlally, anyway?

Blinking, she rubbed her eyes. For an instant she thought she'd spotted Dima – her Dima – striding on the road below. She looked again at the upright old lady with a stick and a straw bag over one shoulder. Minou shook her head. It wasn't Dima at all. Dima had always worn a yellow sari, with her wiry silver hair twisted into a bun. This lady's hair was cropped short and her tucked-up sari was white cotton. Only her fearless stride and straight back reminded Minou of her grandmother. She watched the woman disappear along the mountain road, curving into a copse of pines.

Moments later, two men dressed in black clattered along behind her, riding scrawny grey ponies. Minou heard a low murmur of voices. She stood and watched as they tethered the ponies and tied black scarves over their faces. When they followed the old woman into the pine trees, she decided to wake Jay. She did not like the look of this. Hadn't Malkan warned them about bandits?

'Jay – wake up!'

'Whassit?'

'Bandits – I think they're about to attack an old lady!'

'What? Sparrow, wait – come back!'

But Minou had already run on ahead and was treading light-footed through the trees. She heard Jay grumbling as he caught up with her.

'*Shh!* Look,' she hissed.

Crouching behind a wide tree trunk, they saw one of the men holding a knife to the old lady's throat, while his companion snatched away her bag.

'Go!' Jay whispered.

With a running leap, Minou dived upon the man with the knife, letting out a cry of rage. How dare they? Cowards – attacking a helpless old lady! She threw a flying kick to the bandit's fist, sending his knife spinning, and whirled to punch him in the side. Her opponent roared and lumbered forward, reaching for her neck with his great hairy hands. She leaped clear with a handspring, flipping on to her feet and kicked him hard in the ribs, half-winding him. Rolling free, she grabbed his knife from where it lay on the ground and spun to face him, gripping it tight.

Jay had disarmed the other thief and was standing over him while the old lady, unharmed by her ordeal, whacked at him with her walking stick. She pulled out a large whistle hanging from a cord around her neck and sounded an ear-splitting blast.

'Help is on its way!' she announced breathlessly.

But the bandits had had enough and were stumbling off into the trees. Then they heard a canter of hooves, as the thieves fled on horseback. The old lady smiled broadly at Minou and Jay. 'Well – that was an adventure! May the Lady's blessings fall upon you like rain, young ones. Thank you for your help.'

'It was nothing,' Jay told her.

'We had fun!' Minou added.

'These bandits can be so troublesome. I am very

much against violence, but sometimes it can't be helped! Here comes my carriage. I have a stiff knee, only walked for the exercise.'

Minou and Jay stared as a small wagon pulled by two sturdy mountain ponies jingled around the curving road. It was made from woven cane, like an oversized basket, the open door screened with yellow silk hangings.

'Milly, what happened? We heard your whistle!' a voice exclaimed as a slim hand pulled back the curtain. 'I told you not to walk by yourself.'

'Nothing at all! I fell and these wonderful young people helped me up,' the old woman cried. 'May blessings fall on them like rain,' she added, climbing into the carriage.

Minou repeated her words, the scent of trodden pine needles rising around her. *May the Lady's blessings fall upon them like rain.* It was something Dima might have said. Not everyone in Moonlally remembered that monsoon rains were brought by the Lady. She watched the funny little woven carriage, pulled by its stout ponies, clip away and disappear over the summit of the hill. She was still holding the bandit's knife. Wiping the blade clean, she tucked it into her waistband. It might come in useful.

Twenty-seven

'Sparrow, there you go again. Running off to rescue another stray!' Jay shook his head.

Minou rounded on him as they walked back to the temple, suddenly cross. It had been *her* idea to find the Queen, not Jay's. Besides, wasn't helping old ladies and baby elephants what made the Green Orchids different from the General? 'Maybe I am a wild dog, after all,' she began. 'But, Jay – who would you rather have on your side, a dog or a cobra? Wouldn't a dog be more loyal?'

'Eh? Not the cobras and dogs again!'

She scowled at him. 'I'm only repeating what you said. That day, by the river.'

'I say a lot of things. But wasn't she a funny old thing? You don't often see women with short hair like that unless—' Jay froze on the path and turned to her. 'Unless they're nuns.'

'What?'

'*Nuns!* By the Lady and her thundering elephants, I'll bet that woman we rescued is one of the nuns. Let's find Farisht and follow her – she'll take us to wherever the Queen's in hiding.'

As Jay spoke, a blast of gunfire broke apart the peaceful scene. Music drifting from the temple was drowned out by angry shouts and frightened screams. They exchanged glances.

'What was that?'

But Jay was already running down the slope. They skirted the food tent and hurried through the gardens, all the while dodging crowds of pilgrims, milling about in confusion. Jay stopped dead. 'Wait, Sparrow,' he whispered. 'Look—'

Directly ahead stood the policeman they'd seen in Karomsheel market. And he wasn't alone – behind stood a line of police, each wearing the khaki uniform and red kepi hat of the Moonlally force.

'What's going on?' Minou asked a woman standing close by, a child on her hip. 'Why are the police here?'

'Isn't it terrible – and during a festival too! They said there were reports of a dangerous fugitive at the temple. We had to leave, then we heard gunshots. I expect he tried to escape.'

They looked at each other in horror.

'Jay, we need to find Farisht!'

He nodded. 'Let's get out of the gardens – we can't move for the crowds. We'll go round the side of the temple.'

They made slow progress, pushing against the pilgrims, many still in elaborate costumes. Finally skirting the temple complex, they came face to face with a line of policemen. People were still being herded out to the forecourt.

'Try to get to the entrance!' Jay called over the heads of the crowd.

'You two, keep clear!' a policeman barked, brandishing his truncheon. 'The festival's being closed down. We have a fugitive under armed guard. Stand back!'

Minou and Jay exchanged worried glances. They shrank into the crowd as the Commandant of Whitetown strode from the temple in his safari jacket. He had removed his pith helmet, loosened his top buttons and was mopping his bald scalp with a handkerchief. 'Disperse this crowd of gaping fools – the heathen festival is over!' he shouted, ginger moustache twitching.

'Sir. *Yes, sir!*' a policeman replied.

Minou gasped. Behind the Commandant, she could see Farisht being dragged from the temple. His yellow shirt was blood-stained, and he was handcuffed between two policemen.

She ran towards him, calling his name.

'Take him in!' The Commandant glared at her furiously, his face pink as a slab of boiled ham. 'Get back girl! Wait. Why, you're the spitting image—'

'Where are you taking my friend?' Minou interrupted him. She felt so helpless, watching the policemen bundle Farisht into a police car, she didn't care if the Commandant recognised her.

'How dare you question me?' The man stared at her, his face twitching with anger. 'You're the Shadow, aren't you? Fugitive from the *Napoleon* – have her arrested!' he shouted.

Minou backed away from the Commandant. The deep growl of an engine sounded. Someone called her name and she turned. Jay, wearing a wooden mask of the elephant god, rode up on a black motorcycle with sidecar.

'Sparrow – jump in!' he yelled, skidding to a stop beside her.

'*Get them!* Useless bunch of fools!' the Commandant thundered at his men.

Minou sidestepped to dodge one policeman, shaking off another who'd grabbed her arm. She tumbled backwards into the sidecar, and with an ear-splitting revving of the engine they were off, Jay circling the motorbike around the grounds to head up the road that led into the hills.

'There are too many pilgrims around for them to shoot. Don't worry!' Jay yelled.

'I'm not!' Minou yelled back. They were rattling along the bumpy ground so fast that her teeth felt loose in her head.

A gunshot sounded. The policemen were giving chase. They jolted along the stony road up the slope, to a crackle of half-hearted firing from the men. This was where they'd seen the old nun disappear in her little carriage. Jay drove with skill; they'd soon outpaced the police, whose cars couldn't manage the narrow track.

'Are they behind us?' Jay shouted.

Minou twisted around to check. 'I can't see anyone.'

'Right.' Jay swerved to a stop and pulled off his mask. He slipped from the back of the motorcycle and Minou unfolded herself from the sidecar.

'By the Lady,' she breathed. 'The look on that Commandant's face when you drove up in the elephant-god mask! Where did you find this contraption, Jay?'

The boy grinned. 'The motorcycle? I found it parked by the temple entrance. I'm pretty sure it belongs to the Commandant. Quick, let's get off-road and head overland that way – it'll be harder for them to track us down.' He pointed to a swathe of long grass carpeting the steep hill beyond a stream.

'We can't leave Farisht – what will they do to him?' Minou called as they splashed across the shallow stream to climb the slope.

'They'll take him to Moonlally. But we must keep going, Sparrow. We need to reach the Queen, before the Commandant works out what we're doing here. We're fugitives now.'

'He recognised me,' she told him. 'But he didn't see your face, and Farisht won't talk.'

'Sparrow, you saw what happened to Tal and Little, didn't you? The Moonlally police are merciless. We must find the Queen quickly – Farisht would say the same.'

Minou sighed. 'I wish we had the map.'

'Too dangerous to go back for it. Can you remember anything – any landmarks?'

Minou pictured the map she'd studied so often. She saw the temple at Narsin with its elaborate tiers and spires and the silver path beyond, winding up a blue peak, like the one they climbed now. 'The shape of this hill seems familiar. I think we're going the right way.'

The sun had set. Minou felt a chill in the night breeze. As they climbed the grassy slope, she looked back to check the police were no longer in pursuit. They took a zigzag path, scrambling over rocks so they'd be harder to track. By the time they'd reached the summit, a full white moon shone in the deepening blue sky. Before them, the ground levelled to a wide plain, moonlight spilling silver over the wind-stirred grass. Under its bright gleam, they could make out faint white shapes in the distance.

Minou pointed. 'That's it! The place marked on the map – the old shrines where the nuns live.' She remembered the story Farisht had told them. This was where Moonlally's queen had prayed for a daughter, before transforming into the Dark Lady, and gaining the third eye's powers.

Far below, lights winked in the velvet night, marking the site of Narsin temple. Minou's heart ached when she thought of Farisht, dragged off by the police, frightened and alone. Where was he now? Locked in a jail cell – or worse? She tried to shake off her fears. If the Queen returned, the people would revolt against the General's rule. Soon, all his prisoners would be free.

Twenty-eight

'This can't be the place – it's deserted,' Jay objected.

'But it has to be.' Minou pointed. 'Look at those small buildings. They're just like the ones on the map.'

They walked on, gradually drawing nearer to the domed white shrines dotted over the scrubby plain. The night sky had become overcast, a full moon faintly visible through the clouds. Jay found some dry kindling and used Minou's knife and a stone to spark a flame. Lighting a branch to use as a torch, they searched one empty shrine after another. They saw scattered animal droppings and tiny scuttling lizards, but no sign of human life.

'*Hello?*' Minou called. Only a faint, ghostly echo answered.

Jay shrugged. 'This is hopeless, Sparrow. It's abandoned. Miss Ophelia's information was a guess. The Queen's long gone – that's if she was ever here at all.'

Minou slumped to the ground, disappointed. Could Jay be right? Had the nuns vanished, and the Queen with them? Was Ophelia mistaken? But then she remembered the old lady they'd saved from the bandits. A strange feeling of certainty seized her. She shivered. 'You've forgotten that nun, Jay – in her funny little carriage. Even if this isn't the place, it must be in this direction.'

Jay glanced down at her. 'I hope you're right, Sparrow. But it's pitch-black and we're both tired. Let's sleep in one of the shrines and go on searching tomorrow.'

They gathered dried grass and twigs for a meagre fire and bedded down uncomfortably on the cold floor. Minou had forgotten to recite the Lady's song that morning, the one Farisht had taught her. Tonight, lost in the hills, her friend far away, she comforted herself by whispering it, as she fell into an uneasy sleep.

Deep in the night, Minou was tugged from her dreams by an unearthly light filtering into the shrine. She shook off her stiffness and tiptoed outside. An owl swooped overhead, its haunting call shattering the night's hushed still. She felt a breeze stir the long grass and inhaled deeply. There it was – that familiar scent of rain on dry earth. In the distance thunder rumbled. Before her, the black night seemed to gather and shape itself into the outline of a woman, her eyes glowing like twin embers. The Dark Lady, whose third eye shone out with a radiance brighter than moonlight, turning the dew-soaked ground silver.

Minou dropped to her knees, folding her hands in prayer. If she'd ever needed the Dark Lady's help, it was now. They were lost in the hills, with no map to lead them to the Queen. She sang the hymn Farisht had taught her. To her surprise, she felt the tin elephant growing warm at her throat.

> *'Dark Lady, born of the clouded hills,*
> *whose songs summon the rains down still,*
> *whose third eye spears as lightning strike,*
> *whose powers turn back the highest tide.*
> *Your radiance rivals the silver moon,*
> *your anger brings tempest with monsoon.*
> *Grant us blessings in pearls from oceans deep.*
> *May your amber gaze heal those that weep.*
> *Beloved of poets, weavers of words,*
> *your soft voice tames wild elephant herds.*
> *When the floodwaters rise at year thirteen,*
> *to renew red earth and clothe her green,*
> *then anoint our queendom's rightful queen.'*

The figure of the Dark Lady drifted between the shrines, the light from her brow casting a luminous path. Minou followed, stumbling over rocky ground to keep up, until she was well beyond the plain. The tin elephant at her throat was now burning hot, almost searing her skin. She pulled it off and ran, the string looped round her wrist.

The ground dipped suddenly and Minou tumbled, banging her head on a rock. She rolled on to her back, rubbing her forehead ruefully. Dragging herself upright, she looked around. She was alone in a clearing between huge trees that whispered overhead. The darkness had lifted; patches of sky showed deep blue between black leaves. On the horizon, a band of sunrise glowed pale orange.

The Dark Lady had vanished, as suddenly as she'd appeared. How would she find her way back to Jay? Too tired to think any more, Minou yawned and curled herself up on the damp earth to sleep.

Minou woke hours later to find herself warm and dry, blankets heaped over her. She was lying on a mattress, the floor rising and dipping with a gentle sway that reminded her of Dima's shack on the river. A greenish light seeped through the walls, woven from strips of wood.

A young nun with cropped hair, dressed in a white sari, was sitting by her on a low stool. She bent over Minou. There was something familiar in her beautiful face, narrow eyes and high cheekbones.

'How are you feeling?' the woman asked, concern in her voice.

'I told you,' another voice proclaimed. 'Said she was a tough little thing, didn't I? She's all right!'

'You did, Milly,' the young woman agreed.

'It's you!' Minou smiled, pleased to see the old nun they'd saved from the bandits. She uncurled her arms and legs, yawned and stretched, pushing herself up from the floor.

'I'm here on an important mission,' she told them. 'I need to speak with the Queen of Moonlally. I know she's living with you nuns.'

The two women exchanged looks and the older one shook her head. 'Child,' she asked. 'Who *are* you? And what do you know of the Queen of Moonlally?' She pressed a clay cup of tea into Minou's hands. 'Drink up!' she told her.

Minou took a gulp of tea, which had no milk, but tasted fresh and sweet. 'I'm Minou, or Sparrow, and I have a message for the Queen. The Green Orchids – they're rebels, trying to overthrow the General – want her to return to Moonlally.'

The young woman frowned. 'What makes you think the Queen is alive? I heard Moonlally's queen died years ago.'

'She is alive, by the Lady! She escaped the palace, but the General told everyone she was dead. He had a wax figure buried in her coffin. I heard it from Shri, the clockmaker.'

The young woman's eyes widened. 'Shri?' she whispered. She reached across to open a woven bamboo blind. Green light flooded the cabin. From the window, Minou saw they were high above ground – the wooden hut was perched in the branches of a great tree. She turned back to see the two women staring at her.

'What's your *real* name, child?' the old woman asked.

'Mignon Moonshine's the name my Dima gave me. She adopted me after I was found by the river on the night of the great storm, thirteen years ago. What's wrong?'

The younger woman had let out a cry, her expression tender and terrible.

'What is it? Why are you looking at me like that?'

'This amulet – tell us where you found it,' the old woman said, holding out the tin elephant. Minou's hand flew to her bare neck. She reached for it but the old woman snatched it away.

'That's mine! It belonged to my mother.'

'It's true you had it clutched in your fist when we found you last night. But what's inside this silver elephant belongs to the Dark Lady and no one else.'

'But there's nothing *inside* – it's only a battered tin elephant,' Minou protested.

The younger nun took the amulet from the older woman and prised at the seam soldered along its belly. 'I'll try to open it, but the mechanism's worn!' she said with a frown, taking a pin from the drape of her sari. 'Thirteen times against the clock.' She counted quietly under her breath.

'The child kept it safe; I'll say that,' the old lady muttered.

Minou frowned, confused. 'Kept *what* safe? I don't understand.'

'Look, it's moving – even though it's old and tarnished. Shri's workmanship was always so wonderful.' The young nun finished turning the pin in the belly of the elephant. With a small click, the head lifted off. She shook out a tiny bundle of yellowed silk and started to unwrap it.

The old nun let out a cackle of delight. 'May the Lady's blessings fall upon us like rain! Look, child – do you know what this is?'

Minou stared at the black, teardrop-shaped jewel that lay on the young nun's palm. It caught the soft light of the cabin with a smoky radiance, specks of gold glittering like constellations of tiny stars.

The young nun looked at Minou, her huge eyes liquid. 'The third eye of the Dark Lady,' she whispered. 'I didn't think I'd ever see it again.'

Astonished, Minou glanced between them. She didn't understand. How had her grandmother come to possess the third eye of the Dark Lady? The young woman placed her hand over Minou's – it was soft, not calloused as bark, like old Dima's.

'Do you know who I am, child? Or rather – who I was?'

Minou looked at her large eyes and high cheekbones. She was beautiful, even with the starkly cropped hair. She knew that face, from the icon of the Dark Lady in Shri's temple. Unable to speak, she nodded.

The nun's voice fell. 'I have lived as a nun for almost thirteen years. But long ago, in another life, I was known as Queen Ambra of Moonlally.'

Twenty-nine

A cascade of bells rang out as if in celebration. Minou gazed in shock, as the nun's – no, the *Queen's* words – sunk in. She'd done it! They had all done it together: Minou, Jay, Farisht and Ophelia. Found the Queen of Moonlally, alive and well. For a moment, she couldn't speak. Tears flooded her eyes and she blinked them away furiously. Now, they could return to Moonlally – she and Jay – and tell the other Green Orchids of the Queen's return. Soon, Moonlally would be free of the General's rule.

The Queen struggled to her feet. Taking up an ivory-handled stick, she made for the door of the cabin, Minou stood to follow her.

'Wait!' The old lady caught her ankle with a surprisingly strong grip. 'Those bells are the alarm signal. Don't move until we see who's out there.'

'Another visitor, would you believe? A young man this time,' the Queen called.

'That's Jay, he's with me!' Minou pulled herself free and scrambled towards the door. She found herself standing beside the Queen on the balcony of a treehouse. Wooden stairs wound around the massive trunk to the ground. She looked about to see other mossy tree trunks with cabins clinging to them, almost vanishing into the rustling green canopy of leaves. So this was the village where the nuns lived. Hidden high in the treetops – no wonder she hadn't seen them at night. Voices echoed from the clearing below. She squinted down to see Jay, a white-clad nun either side of him. The nuns on surrounding balconies had drawn their bows and arrows, all aimed at her friend and ready to fire.

'*Stop*. Please don't shoot!'

'Sisters!' Queen Ambra called in a clear voice. 'Lower your weapons. Silence the alarm bells.' The nuns lowered their bows.

'We have to be wary of bandits in this remote place,' the Queen explained. 'That's why we first moved into the trees from the shrines. We're well-trained in archery, so they rarely bother us now.'

'Jay's not a bandit, he's with me,' Minou told her. 'We came to find you together. For the rebels – the Green Orchids.'

The Queen placed a hand on Minou's shoulder. 'You and I have so much to talk about,' she said. 'But we'll have to wait a little longer. It's time for morning prayers.'

Below, the nuns were assembling on the grassy clearing. The elder nuns, their faces wrinkled as walnuts, sat cross-legged on straw mats, murmuring sonorous chants for peace. Minou and Jay watched as morning meditation followed, the silence broken only by rustling leaves and the faint tinkle of prayer bells.

After prayers, Queen Ambra asked them for news of Moonlally. She knew of the people's suffering under the General's tyrannical rule, but not of their band of Blacktown rebels, the Green Orchids. The Queen was thoughtful. 'Forgive me,' she said after a moment. 'My life here is so quiet. I haven't spoken to anyone from Moonlally in years and did not know of the resistance to the General. But I still don't understand how you found me. Where did you get this map?'

'From the General's daughter, Ophelia. She's a rebel – determined to help us overthrow him,' Minou told her.

'The General's daughter is brave, as I must be. If you think my return will help defeat the regime, then return I shall.'

'If you do, Queen Ambra, all Blacktown will support you,' Jay broke in. 'The Commandant can't stand in our way. He knows you're the true heir.'

The Queen sighed. 'Our beautiful queendom,' she said. 'Small, fierce and forever under attack. When Whitetowners first came to Indica, we needed weapons for protection, so we traded with them –' she shook her head – 'before we go further, I must speak to the elders of our community. Only they know of my former life.'

The younger nuns departed with baskets to their tea plantation high in the hills, while Queen Ambra sat deep in conversation with the elders. Minou wished they would hurry – the sooner they left for Moonlally,

the sooner they could free the General's prisoners –
Tal, Little and Farisht. With a shudder, she thought of
the crocodiles in the palace moat.

Jay sensed her impatience and suggested they run
through their kalari exercises in the clearing. 'This
is going to be the biggest fight of our lives, Sparrow.
We'll need to be on good form.'

They were about to begin sparring, when to her
surprise, Jay let his fists fall to his side and bowed.
Minou turned to see the Queen, leaning on her ebony
walking stick. She wore a simple white sari, her narrow
feet were bare and her face calm.

'No need for bowing and ceremony,' she told Jay. 'I
renounced my title long ago. Please, would you excuse
us? I'd like to speak with Minou alone.' She smiled
at Minou. 'A stream flows beyond those trees. It's
pleasant there – will you join me? And tell me about
yourself as we walk.'

Minou followed the Queen along the path into the
green cave of forest. She told her how, after Dima's
death, she'd been taken to the palace as Miss Ophelia's
shadow. The Queen was astonished at her adventures,
particularly their winged escape from the airship. They
paused at the stream's crossing point.

'I'm sorry for all the trials you faced finding me,
Minou. I thank the Lady for keeping you safe.'
The Queen pointed at the grey stepping stones that
bridged the sparkling waters. 'This stream is sacred
to the Dark Lady. After she came to the hills, she
discarded all ornaments, except for a single string

of Moonlally pearls. When she needed to cross, she flung them in and they became stepping stones.' She turned to Minou and smiled. 'This place is filled with our history. But I'm talking too much. What did your grandmother tell you about the silver elephant?'

Minou shrugged. 'I thought it was a tin toy. Dima said it was in my crib when I was found on the riverbank – that it belonged to my mother. And Dima never lied.' It was true, Dima did not lie. But perhaps she'd found the elephant herself, and made up a story to please Minou when she was small?

'No...' the Queen said hesitantly. 'She didn't lie. It was in your cradle, and it did belong to your mother.'

They both stared into the rippling stream. Leaves drifted down from the canopy above, floating away on the current. Minou shook her head. 'But I don't understand. How did the Dark Lady's third eye end up in the elephant?'

The Queen bit her lip. 'I put it there. The third eye is a black diamond, a rare fragment of fallen star.' She turned to Minou, her delicate face lit with love. 'Milly brought it to me on the night I fled the palace. It has special powers – I hoped it might protect you.'

'Protect *me*?' Minou, unable to meet the Queen's gaze, stared at the stream, dappled in light. It gurgled over the rocks; a song so different from the deep swell of the Lally. 'But why?'

The Queen kneeled to trail her hands in the stream. She turned to Minou, tears in her eyes, and sprinkled her forehead with tiny droplets of water. 'Minou. *You* were the reason I left the palace,' she said quietly. 'I gave birth to you on the night of the great storm, almost thirteen years ago. The city was flooded. I asked Tomas to smuggle you to safety and jumped from my balcony, injuring my ankle.'

The Queen flourished her stick. 'Milly helped me to Blacktown Cemetery. We hid in a tomb until I'd healed, then escaped to the hills. She wrote to Tomas, telling him I was safe and asking him to bring you to me. Her letter was returned unopened, with a note to say he had drowned that night in the Lally. There was no mention of a baby at all.'

'I made a terrible mistake, leaving you. But I had no choice. You are a queen of Moonlally. The General would have killed us both. To this day, he does not know that I had – that I *have* a child.' The Queen wiped her eyes with her sari. 'I thought I'd lost you for ever, but the Dark Lady has brought you back to me. It's a miracle!'

Minou gazed into the Queen's anguished face. She'd found the Queen, and the Queen was her mother. They were the same person. She shook her head in confusion. 'But I don't want to be queen – I'd be no good at all. I can't even do a proper curtsey.'

The Queen gave a half-sobbing laugh. 'I know how you feel,' she said. 'I didn't want to be queen either. But we have a fight ahead of us – the General won't yield power easily. You and I must work together to defeat him.'

'But why me?' Minou cried. 'How do I matter?'

The Queen gazed into the running stream. 'The Dark Lady, the queen and heir,' she told her. 'We three form a sacred bond that protects Moonlally. We're the only queendom in all Indica – perhaps in the world! When my mother died, I was too young to stand up to the General and Commandant. That's when our troubles began.'

A high, whooping call sounded from the canopy above. Her mother pointed at a black bird with ruby eyes, perched on a low branch. 'A *koel!* The Dark Lady's bird, you know. When you hear that call, the rains are approaching.' She smiled at Minou. 'It's a good sign. The song of the Lady has this prophecy. *When floodwaters rise at year thirteen, to renew red earth and paint her green. Then anoint our queendom's rightful queen.*'

Thoughts whirled in Minou's mind, as birds flocked from the trees in alarm to circle the clearing. She stared up at the sky in horror. A deep rumbling shook the air and the vast black shadow of the airship yawned over the forest.

'The *Napoleon!*' she whispered. 'By the Lady. It's the General's airship!'

Thirty

The purple balloon hovered above them, the gondola dangling so low the treetops bent beneath its weight.

'Run and hide!' The Queen gripped Minou's arm. 'I can't lose you again. We can deal with this. Our sisters are armed – they'll bring the balloon down with their arrows.'

Alarm bells rang from treetop cabins as the nuns gathered on their balconies, weapons aimed at the airship. Minou started as a gunshot cracked across the clearing, a line of smoke twisting from one of the treehouses.

'By the Lady, who's firing the gun?'

'Milly!' the Queen exclaimed. 'She owns an ancient firearm – she'll injure herself. Would you stop her? But be careful!'

Minou sprinted towards the treehouse and flew up the steps. The old woman was crouched on the balcony, holding a pistol above her head.

Jay stood beside her. 'Milly, listen. The hydrogen gas inside the balloon will explode if you fire a gun at it!' he explained patiently. 'And with this old relic, you'll probably blow us all up first!'

'If they've come for the Queen, they'll have to get past me, I tell you!' Milly lowered the pistol reluctantly.

'The Queen's safe – she's in the woods,' Minou told her. 'What shall we do now, Jay? How did they find us out here?'

The boy looked up at the *Napoleon*'s purple balloon looming above the green canopy. 'I don't know. But we're all right – there's not enough space to land an airship in this clearing.'

As they watched, a heavy rope was flung from the gondola, unfurling among the trees. Jay whistled under his breath. 'The captain knows they can't descend any further. They've slung a towrope down to anchor. I'll see what's going on – you stay here!' He leaped down the treehouse steps and into the clearing.

Minou stared at the knotted rope swinging between the trees. The main door of the gondola opened and a white shape leaned out. She blinked. Could it really be?

'Jay, I think that's Ophelia!' she shouted, hurrying from the tree house. She skirted a group of tea-pickers, their baskets brimming with leaves and hurtled towards the boy, who had grabbed the heavy towrope. 'Please don't shoot!' she called to the nuns, standing with arrows poised. '*Ophelia!* What are you doing here?'

'*Sparrow!*' Ophelia called happily. 'I've come to collect the Queen – and you too! Can someone secure the towrope?'

Minou nodded to Jay, who fastened it securely to a broad-trunked pine.

'Crew, lower the rope ladder,' Ophelia ordered. 'Her Majesty will climb aboard – we must return to Moonlally immediately!'

A rope ladder swung down from the gondola and Jay seized it. 'Who else is on board?' he demanded of the General's daughter. 'How do we know this isn't a trap?'

'No danger of that – I checked the crew were loyal to the cause!' Ophelia shouted in reply, above the deep thrumming of the engine.

Jay hauled himself on and shimmied swiftly up the ladder. 'Wait here!' he called to Minou. 'I'll make sure it's safe.'

The Queen leaned upon her cane as she walked slowly out of the copse of trees, gazing at the airship in wonder. She joined Minou; together they held the swaying rope ladder steady.

'Your Majesty!' Ophelia waved. 'It's really you.'

'Sparrow!' Jay called down. 'It's safe to board.'

'Quick, Sparrow,' Ophelia urged. 'Help Her Majesty climb the ladder and board. The monsoon's close behind and that towrope won't anchor us for long.'

A wild gust of air swung through the clearing, rocking the treetops. Minou took her mother's hands. 'Will you come with us – back to Moonlally?' she asked.

'How I wish I could! But I can't climb with my bad leg. You go on – Milly and I will follow overland. I'll hold the ladder steady with the other nuns – come, sisters!'

Minou bit her lip. 'I don't want to leave you. But the police took my friend, Farisht. I must see that he's safe.' She hugged her mother and started climbing. Halfway up the ladder, she glanced down at the forest clearing, to see the nuns gathered around the Queen. *Her mother.* How strange those words sounded. The nuns were calling out – she strained to hear their soft voices over the rising wind.

As she reached the door, Jay held out his hand and hauled her into the gondola, where she collapsed on to the floor. 'Jay, the Queen,' she told him breathlessly. 'She can't climb the rope ladder because of her bad leg.'

Jay pointed to the nuns, who'd suspended one of the tea baskets from the ladder. The crew were winching it in, straining against its weight. Curled inside the basket as it jerked unsteadily upwards, was the Queen of Moonlally.

Minou helped her mother to her feet. The Queen was pale and shaken, her sari crumpled and leaves caught in her hair. 'I couldn't do it,' she said, her face stricken. 'I couldn't let you go – not again!' She hugged Minou to her. 'I left my stick on the ground, may I take your arm?'

Together, they made their way to the viewing lounge, stumbling as the gondola rocked beneath them. The nuns had untied the towrope, the crew hauled it in, and with a deep growl of its engines, the *Napoleon* lifted into the air, shedding ballast to gain height until they were well above the forest. The clamour of bells from the village faded as they drifted over the hills.

'What a strange contraption!' the Queen said. 'I must say a prayer for our journey.' She lowered herself into a chair and closed her eyes. 'What do you see out there, Minou? Are the skies still clear?'

Minou hurried to the windows of the viewing lounge. The sky outside was charcoal, an unruly wind blustered around the great balloon. She pressed her fingertips to the glass, patterned with pulsing raindrops. The air smelled electric, like before a storm. Under her feet, the floor of the gondola rolled and pitched, as thunder drummed low, followed by a flash of lightning.

The Queen gripped the sides of her chair. 'I don't like the sound of that,' she said. 'I fear the monsoon is close.'

A great clap of thunder boomed. Minou gasped. A mass of black clouds reared ahead like a mountain, lightning flashing, pale and eerie within. Rain pounded at the windows, as fast and loud as temple drums. The monsoon was upon them, and it was gaining power.

'Minou, you must see if your friends need help. I can't imagine this thing holds up well in a storm.'

'Are you sure you'll be all right?' Minou asked. Her mother nodded. They heard Ophelia call up the stairs. 'All hands on deck!'

Minou bolted down to join her. Helmsmen, riggers and navigators scurried about, following the captain's orders. 'Quick!' Ophelia beckoned her past the navigation room, where Jay manned the instruments. 'Captain needs us. Reporting for duty, sir!'

'Steady the helm,' the captain told them, pointing at the gilded wooden wheel that steered the airship. Ophelia grasped one spoke, Minou another. 'Monsoon's on us like an angry tiger. We need the airship to descend, but if we vent too much and lightning strikes, we'll go up like fireworks. Keep her even, young lady!' he cried as Minou tugged harder and the wheel swung towards her. Both girls gripped the helm, bracing against each other's weight.

'Here she comes!' he shouted.

Storm winds screamed along the surface of the balloon, which juddered with their force. The gale seized the tethers that lashed the gondola, shaking the cabin like a giant hand. Minou's feet slid from under her but she kept hold of the helm.

'Nose down!' the captain shouted to the pitchmen either side, spinning wheels to keep the ship level. 'Turn off the valves!'

The storm howled around them, blacking out the windows. Rain pounded and spat, needles swung and rattled wildly. The wheel bucked like a live thing under Minou's grasp.

'Steering light on!' the captain commanded. The yellow path of light appeared before them, piercing black air. 'Tailwinds!' he added. 'Hang on tight!'

The helm dragged Minou's aching arms, as the winds tore along the airship's bloated balloon. She screwed her eyes up in effort, hanging on with all her strength as thunderclaps fractured the air.

'We're all going to die!' Ophelia wailed.

'No, we're not!' Minou yelled back.

'Keep below the storm and we're in with a chance!' the captain shouted. 'Provided the updraught doesn't get us,' he added.

The cabin lights went off. Cries rang from the crew as the airship plunged sickeningly downwards. Minou's ears popped with the change in air pressure. She gripped the helm, knees and elbows locked as the ship floored, buffeted by the updraught. Ophelia was thrown free, crumpling to the floor. For a long moment, Minou steadied the wheel alone. *Don't let go*, she told herself, gritting her teeth.

'Ballast off!' the captain barked, reaching over to take the helm. 'We've done it.'

'By the *Lady*,' Minou gasped, rubbing her eyes. Outside, grey clouds dwindled in the distance and the skies were clearing. Her ears rang, but the howling winds had fallen silent. The *Napoleon* had made it through the storm.

IV

Return to Moonlally

Queen Kali, Lightning Striker

Our first and greatest Queen Kali, who became the Dark Lady, was granted the power to spear lightning bolts from her third eye. Though she only used her gift upon sworn enemies, her advisors were nervous when delivering bad news. They preferred to place such messages on the back of her daughter's pet tortoise, Kurma, who knew to retreat into its shell at the first sign of sparks.

From *A True History of the Queens of Moonlally*

Thirty-one

'Wasn't that something – steering an airship through a storm!' Jay grinned at Minou and Ophelia from behind his barometers and compasses. Both girls had collapsed in an exhausted heap in a corner of the navigation room.

'It was something all right – I'm not sure what!' Minou groaned, scrambling to her feet. 'Can I look?' she asked, pointing to his telescope.

'Of course, Sparrow. Twist this brass wheel to focus. That storm spun us around, but we're back on course.'

Minou gazed down at the passing landscape. The airship's black shadow drifted over blue hills and green valleys fissured with streams. They had reached the plateau of abandoned shrines and moved slowly over the pale pink temple at Narsin, its carved pagoda soaring to meet them. Crowds massed around the temple, turning wondering faces up to the *Napoleon*. She searched the sea of people for Farisht's lean figure. Maybe – just maybe – the police had let him go? As the airship floated over slopes patched with gold sunshine, she let out a cry. Suddenly, she saw sunlight wink from a pile of shattered glass and splintered wood, half-hidden in the undergrowth.

'Laxmi!' she whispered. 'And Luna.'

That was where they'd hidden Laxmi the elephant and Farisht's magic lantern. Now both were smashed to smithereens – and worse, the map of the nuns' village was inside Luna's case. What if the police found it?

'*Sparrow!*' Ophelia called. 'We're needed above deck. The Queen has summoned us.'

The Queen, seated in the viewing lounge, looked up as they approached. 'Thank the Dark Lady you're all safe – what is it?' she asked Minou, scanning her anxious face. 'What's wrong?'

'I think the police have found the map of the nuns' village. We must warn them.'

The Queen nodded. 'When we land, I'll telegraph the priest at Narsin – he's a friend. But I still don't understand how you found this map.'

'It was among your letters to Tomas.' Ophelia flushed. 'Shri told me he was your only visitor, and that you wrote to him every day. I wanted to discover where you lived in exile – I tried not to read anything personal.'

'*Tomas!*' The Queen's face lit up with an expression of mingled joy and pain.

'Yes – Father Jacob kept all his possessions locked in a trunk. He hadn't opened it since Tomas's death. I begged him to give me the letters.'

The Queen smiled sadly. 'Friends,' she began, turning to clasp Minou's hand. 'My daughter and I must speak with you.'

Jay looked at Minou. '*Daughter!* Did I miss something?'

Minou pushed a lounge chair towards him. 'You might want to sit down to hear this,' she said, curling herself at her mother's feet.

'By the third eye of the Dark Lady, I swear Minou is my own daughter,' the Queen told them. 'She was born almost thirteen years ago, at the time of the last great floods. I was the General's prisoner. Tomas was my only visitor and—'

'Father Jacob told me he saved my life...' Minou broke in. But there was so much Father Jacob hadn't known.

The Queen squeezed Minou's hand. 'I'm ashamed to tell you brave young people, but the thought of returning to Moonlally fills me with fear. When I was locked up, I'd have gone mad without Tomas's visits. We talked of art, books and music – we even danced!'

'The music box,' Minou whispered, remembering the tiny waltzing figures. She bit her lip. 'I found a music box, in your old room...'

Her mother smiled. 'Shri smuggled it in – we didn't dare play a gramophone. Tomas and I were in love, Minou. When we found we were expecting you, I had to escape the palace. The General would have killed us all. I gave birth to you in secret and asked Tomas to smuggle you to safety, the third eye as protection.

Milly and I fled during the storm. Tomas was to bring you to us when it was safe. After he drowned, I thought you were lost for ever. Nothing mattered any more.'

'Tomas was my father?'

The Queen nodded through her tears. Minou rested her head on her mother's lap.

'The lost heir to the throne – the black diamond!' Ophelia gasped. 'It's like an adventure story in a magazine. I knew there was something special about you, Sparrow. So that's why we look alike – we're cousins!'

'The Dark Lady guided you to me for a reason,' the Queen said softly. 'We must restore her third eye, and with it our queendom's protection. Not for us – but for our people. Look!' She untied a knot in her sari to reveal the black diamond, tilting it on her palm to show them its radiant glitter. 'That terrible storm! Without the Dark Lady to guide us, we'd never have survived.'

'Steering the *Napoleon* through a storm was remarkable,' a voice sneered from the doorway. 'But I take the credit myself.' Minou jumped to her feet as the captain stepped into the lounge, brandishing a pistol. 'Hands up, all of you!'

'Captain! What are you doing?' Minou stepped forward.

'Don't move, brat! Unless you want a bullet through you.'

'Do as he says, daughter.' The Queen sounded calm.

'You'd better.' The captain gave a mirthless smile. 'I overheard that touching family reunion. So, the Queen has an heir? The General will be grateful for that information. And for the return of his black diamond.'

'*His* black diamond? It belongs to the Dark Lady!' Anger flashed in Minou's heart, her hands curling into fists. She caught Jay's eye and the boy nodded at the gun in the man's hands.

'Not a step closer, unless you want to see your mother dead!' The captain's voice was icy. 'I'll spare her life – in exchange for the diamond.'

Minou looked at her mother, who sat upright, her face unreadable.

'The third eye of the Dark Lady is sacred.' The Queen spoke steadily. 'You've heard the legend, of course, Captain. If taken by force, bad fortune – even death – is sure to follow.'

'Superstitious nonsense! The General will reward me generously. I'll be a rich man,' he scoffed.

The Queen shrugged. She unknotted the end of her sari drape. 'If you want it so much, take it. Here!' Flashing the black jewel at the captain, she lobbed it through the window.

The man let out an anguished howl at the sound of splintering glass. Minou took advantage of the diversion to let loose a swift kick, jolting the gun from his hand. The gun fired, the bullet grazing her arm to shatter a glass window. Air rushed into the cabin. Jay threw a punch at the captain's stomach and he buckled. Pulling the knife from her waistband – the bandit's knife – Minou held it to his throat, as Jay kneeled to twist the traitor's arms behind him.

'Someone grab that gun from the floor – Ophelia? Make sure the safety's back on!'

'Sparrow, I don't believe this!' Ophelia cried, picking up the gun. 'What a snake!'

'He fooled us both,' Jay told her. 'He must have been a spy for the General from the start – got greedy at the sight of the black diamond!'

'And now it's gone,' Ophelia sighed.

'The third eye of the Dark Lady is perfectly safe.' The Queen stood, her white sari fluttering in the breeze from the broken window. She opened her left hand to show them the jewel nestled in her palm. 'A little trickery – I switched it with a pebble from the tea basket. But, Minou – you're injured!' She sank to the floor beside Minou, who was clutching her left arm, blood seeping through her sleeve.

'It hurts but it's not deep. I can move my arm.'

'I must bandage it.' Her mother ripped away the sleeve of Minou's tunic. 'I'll need the first aid kit, please!' Bunching up her sari, she tore off a length and pressed it against Minou's arm to staunch the bleeding.

Minou winced. 'Jay – I appoint you Captain,' she told him.

'We'd best take care of the old one first,' Jay added. 'I'll have him tied up in the hold for now.'

'Minou,' her mother said softly. 'Daughter, tomorrow is your birthday. Thirteen years since I had you. The Dark Lady's powers are rising – you felt the strength of that storm. You know the words of her hymn?'

Minou nodded. 'I sang it that night we were lost in the hills – the night the Lady guided me to you.'

The Queen smiled. 'We must renew the sacred bond between the queendom and the Dark Lady. I anoint you as my heir – you must be the one to restore her third eye. And before the monsoon reaches Moonlally.'

Minou remembered the heat, pulsing from the tin elephant at her throat and knew the truth of her mother's words. The Dark Lady's deep magic had been with her all along. 'I'll do it,' she agreed. 'Jay, will the *Napoleon* carry us home ahead of the monsoon?'

'It's fast enough – but the balloon's envelope was torn by that gunshot,' Jay told her. 'I can feel us losing height. We'll need to land to patch it up.'

Minou frowned. 'Can we make it as far as Karomsheel?'

Jay nodded. 'That's a plan. We'll land the airship in the market square. Malkan will help – but we'll have to be quick.'

Minou turned. 'Ophelia – does the palace know you're here?'

Ophelia shook her head. 'We were boarding the steamer to Lutetia when we heard. The Baron's been arrested. Charged with murdering his first wife! Didn't I tell you he was a Bluebeard?' She shivered. 'I commandeered the *Napoleon* on its way back and flew straight to Narsin. I spotted the nuns picking tea and knew I had the place.'

'And Mamzelle?' Minou asked her.

'I packed *her* off to Lutetia on the steamer. It's always been her dream!'

'Send the palace a telegram from Karomsheel,' Minou decided. 'Tell them you're on your way home.' She smiled at her friends. Now she knew why she'd felt so happy and carefree on the road with Farisht and Jay. It hadn't only been freedom, but the feeling she belonged.

She understood Dima had her reasons for living alone on the river. Her grandmother had found the secret of Minou's birth, held in the tin elephant with the third eye of the Lady. Fierce as a tiger, Dima had guarded her secret to protect Minou. But she hadn't been right about everything. People weren't tigers – they needed family.

Minou had her people now, and she wasn't going to let anyone take them away.

Thirty-two

As the vast airship approached Moonlally, a powder white moon gleamed in the sky. Minou stood at the helm with Jay, watching the train snake across the plain below, spitting amber sparks into the night. Her mother and Ophelia were safely on board, making their way back to the city.

The *Napoleon* made its final descent, passing over Whitetown's bright boulevards, Blacktown's dim streets, and between the two, the Lally's wide silver curve. Minou could smell the river, a dank, earthy odour ever present in the Moonlally air. She was returning to the palace, not as herself, but disguised as Ophelia, to restore the third eye and the Dark Lady's protection. For the Queen, the people and most of all, for Dima.

Jay steered the airship with skill as the *Napoleon* glided across the city, dropping lower as it approached the mooring mast. They had telegraphed from Karomsheel to warn of their arrival and the landing lights beside the hangar blinked a welcome.

Minou lowered Ophelia's heavy lace veil as the *Napoleon* docked. Her arm was bandaged, it hurt if she moved, but she would keep her pain hidden, at least until she'd reached the temple of the Lady. She heard shouts from the men below as the tethers were made fast. The airship's metal gangway fell into place with a clang, shattering the silence.

She turned to Jay. 'A skilled landing, Captain,' she said, trying to mimic Ophelia's way of speaking.

The boy bowed. 'Why, thank you, Princess.'

Minou rolled her eyes. 'I'm the same old Sparrow, remember?'

'How about Princess Sparrow? Shall I escort you to the ground?'

'Sparrow will be quite satisfactory. Thank you, Captain.'

They strode along the gangplank, Minou wearing Ophelia's slightly too large boots, her petticoats rustling crisply. The elevator grille slid closed and they descended. When it opened, she was relieved to see only a driver and car from the Palace had been sent to take her home.

'We'll meet again soon,' Jay whispered as he helped her into the car. 'I'll head to Blacktown and tell Karu to spread the news of the Queen's return – everyone trusts him. Good night, Miss Ophelia,' he added loudly, for the benefit of the driver.

Minou was taken through the empty streets. She'd often imagined her return to bustling Blacktown, but tonight the city was strangely silent. The General's fortress, too, appeared deserted as they rolled over the moat, past the mechanical guards and lurking crocodiles. A huddle of servants waited by the huge wooden doors to receive her. Minou spoke as little as possible as she followed a maid across the hall, lined with portraits of the General.

'But will you not greet your father and mother?' the girl asked, glancing at a wide marble staircase leading to the General and his wife's apartments.

'Tomorrow. Tell them I am too tired.' The maid looked frightened but nodded. Minou was led through a maze of corridors to the familiar twisting stair leading to Ophelia's tower room.

'I'll manage from here, thank you,' she said, dismissing the girl.

Finally, she dared to throw off her veil. Suppressing a shudder, she entered Ophelia's chamber. The room stirred with circling bats, eager to be out foraging for food. Relieved that her plan did not need her to stay here for long, Minou stepped out of her heavy dress and ripped open the lining. Inside were a hundred, slightly smudged, printed slips of paper.

All poems are messages, Farisht had once told her. Minou hadn't forgotten.

Malkan had been a good friend. All the townspeople of Karomsheel had worked to stitch up the torn silk of the *Napoleon*. They'd left the disgraced captain under lock and key in Malkan's goat shed. And his cousin, who owned the post office, had printed the messages using his small press:

Our queen's alive and has returned, to restore
  the Lady's third eye.
Her enemy to ashes shall burn, as rainstorms
  darken the sky.

Minou knew she wasn't much of a poet – Farisht would have done better. But the scrap of verse, sent at the dead of night, would tell Blacktown of the Queen's homecoming. Ophelia's bats would be her messengers. They flapped restlessly under the rafters of the chamber, clamouring for freedom with high squeals.

She rolled the printed slips into narrow quills, wincing at the pain in her arm. As the bats landed on the table beside her, she slid the quills into their tiny, gnarled claws, recoiling slightly. The creatures were not used to her touch, they hissed and snapped – one bit her finger, leaving tiny beads of red.

Messages dispatched, she searched Ophelia's wardrobe for a set of servants' clothes. Veiled and dressed in white tunic and trousers, the black diamond clasped in her hand, she tiptoed out of the fortress. She eyed the sinister shapes lurking in the water as she scurried across the bridge, hoping the crocodiles had been fed that day.

Minou hurried through the palace, unlocking the gate with Ophelia's keys and slipping silently through. Safe in the shadows, she stopped, waiting for her heart to slow its racing, blood pulsing in her veins. She darted through the crumbling buildings, avoiding moonlit ground. Bats flitted overhead, calling eerily. As she approached Shri's warehouse, the gongs of the palace clocks rang out. It was midnight, which meant it was her thirteenth birthday. She had come at last to the hidden temple of the Dark Lady.

Thirty-three

Despite the late hour, Shri's workshop was alive with activity. Two familiar faces, Tal and Little, were hard at work, polishing twenty-one elephant cannons.

'Tal! How did you make it back here?' The boy looked up and grinned at her.

'Trekked through the jungle, didn't I? Found Little, just like I said I would. The Green Orchids have warned the palace servants, and they're with us. We're ready.'

'How did Little escape?' The other boy glanced up shyly.

'I found him working in the kitchens,' Tal explained. 'He don't like to talk about how he got there.'

Minou gazed around at the ranks of elephants, their mahogany gleaming and brass sparkling. 'Shri, your mechanicals look magnificent!'

Shri bowed to greet her. 'Sparrow, or rather, *Your Highness* – I heard the news. We're preparing for the Queen's arrival. The General ordered a twenty-one-elephant salute in honour of Miss Ophelia's wedding. Little does he know it will welcome our queen home to Moonlally.'

'By the Lady, we'll give him a salute he won't forget! Boom!' Tal added.

A slip of paper fluttered to her feet and Minou swooped to gather it. 'My messages! Those bats haven't dropped them all here, have they?'

'Don't worry, every Blacktowner knows the Queen's on her way,' Tal reassured her.

'We must restore the Lady's third eye!' Shri added. 'Do you have it?'

Minou opened her fist to show him the black diamond.

The old clockmaker's eyes widened. 'Remember, this is no mere jewel but a powerful weapon, one the Dark Lady used to destroy her enemy. We must complete the ceremony. The clouds are gathering, the Dark Lady summons the monsoon rains. Quickly!'

Minou followed Shri into the secret temple. The room was in shadow, the Dark Lady a lonely figure on the raised altar. A cool wind darted in to caress her face, a breath of rain on dry earth fragranced the dank monsoon air. Her hand trembled as she reached up to place the black diamond into the ebony curve of the Lady's forehead. It fitted perfectly. There it was – the greatest treasure in all Moonlally – and Dima had kept it hidden around her neck for years. This was the task she'd returned to the palace for, to restore the Lady's magic and to protect their queendom once more. She folded her hands and kneeled before the icon. 'And now I recite the hymn to the Dark Lady – is that right, Shri?'

The old man nodded. 'Then you may ask for a boon. A secret wish, known only to yourself.'

Minou closed her eyes and started to chant. Her voice, shaky at first, grew stronger with each line:

'Dark Lady… born of the clouded hills,
whose songs summon the rains down still,
whose third eye spears in lightning strike,
whose powers turn back the highest tide.
Your radiance rivals the silver moon,
your anger brings tempest with monsoon—'

She opened her eyes as the scent of rain filled the room. A burst of thunder rolled overhead and she jumped at the sound.

'Here comes the monsoon!' Shri exclaimed. 'Gathering strength with the Lady's growing powers. Continue!'

Minou gazed up at the icon of the Lady, her glance meeting her ruby eyes.

'Grant us blessings as pearls from oceans deep.
May your amber gaze heal those that weep…'

A cannonade of thunder exploded, followed by a crack of lightning that split the black skies open. Alarmed, she sang louder,

'Beloved of poets, weavers of words,
your soft voice tames wild elephant herds.
When floodwaters rise at year thirteen—'

Thunder bouldered, so loud and long that the roofbeams shook. The wind howled, windows rattled and bats shrieked from the high ceiling. A spinning vortex of darkness rose, finer than sand, blacker than dust, shaping into the form of the Dark Lady and drifting towards the carved wooden icon. Spirit and ebony merged to become one. Pale light streamed from her third eye, flooding the temple in a blue lustre, brighter than moonlight. A rushing sounded in Minou's ears.

'Keep going!' Shri called. 'You must sing it all!'

Minou hesitated. Dizzily, she reached to grasp the base of the altar. Dima's voice rang in her head – the hymn to the Dark Lady her grandmother sang every morning. The song Farisht had taught her in the hills. How could she not remember? She opened her mouth, but the words escaped her. She pressed her hands over her ears as she tried to recall the final lines.

'The rains!' Shri prompted. 'They turn the earth...'

Of course! The line began,

'to renew red earth and clothe her green,
then anoint—'

She gasped and broke off, as she recalled the words she feared.

'Shri – I – I can't.' She forced herself to look into the Lady's ruby eyes, glinting with the fire she'd seen before – in the palace and again in the hills, by the deserted shrines. 'I'm sorry – I don't want to be queen – I'm not *ready*!'

She fled the temple, running blindly into the night. Outside, the sky was violet, faint moonlight seeping from dense black cloud. A crackle of electricity hung in the air; raindrops slammed on to stony ground. Soaked to the skin and shivering, Minou hurried towards the fortress and Ophelia's tower. How she longed to turn the other way – to run back to her old life – to forget she was the Queen's daughter and that one day, she would herself be queen.

The moat was flooded and the crocodiles had emerged, their stumpy forelimbs and toothed jaws resting at the water's edge, their yellow eyes fixed upon her. Minou bolted over the bridge, hurtled to the servants' entrance and stumbled up to Ophelia's apartment. She pulled off her wet clothes and collapsed on the narrow bed, falling at once into a dreamless sleep.

On waking next morning, she flinched at the stink of bat droppings. Then she remembered where she was. The third eye had been restored; she'd seen the Dark Lady's spirit enter the icon. But she'd been afraid to say the final words of the hymn. Would the Dark Lady be angry? She felt a prickle of fear on her skin, still clammy from the storm.

Rising, she walked through the chamber, holding her injured arm, now throbbing painfully. She climbed

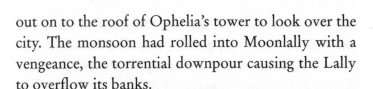

out on to the roof of Ophelia's tower to look over the city. The monsoon had rolled into Moonlally with a vengeance, the torrential downpour causing the Lally to overflow its banks.

Minou gripped the cold stone parapet and leaned forward, staring in shock. The city had flooded. Blacktown's thatched roofs were just visible above the muddy expanse of water below. Small boats plied the streets, rescuing those stranded on rooftops. She worried for the poor and homeless, hoping they had scrambled to safety. Hadn't the Dark Lady's song warned her: *Your anger brings tempest with monsoon?* Had Minou, by disobeying her, caused this destruction?

Gazing down at the murky floodwaters, she tried to imagine another stormy night, thirteen years ago. The night her mother handed her to Tomas, the father she'd never known. She pictured him crossing the flooded river in a rowing boat, bearing his child to safety. The swollen Lally sweeping him away, but hauling her on to its banks, where kindly Father Jacob found her. Did Father Jacob know who she really was?

Dima did, she was sure of it. She'd have opened the silver elephant and found the black diamond. But Dima, like all Moonlally, believed the young queen was dead. Minou's heart ached again at the memory of her grandmother. If only she had lived to see the Queen's triumphant return.

The palace clocks rang out. She leaned further over the parapet to see the gates swing open at a bugle call. Three long and three short notes. The black carriage of the Commandant, pulled by six fine horses, clipped through the flooded courtyard under a grey veil of rain. He was here to visit the General, the man responsible for her father's death and her mother's long exile. The General who had caused so much suffering. His end was near, and Minou wished she could be the one to tell him.

A knock sounded below and she hurried down from the rooftop into the chamber. The maid she'd seen last night crept into the room fearfully. 'Miss... *Ophelia*?' she whispered, staring at Minou in confusion. 'The General has summoned you to an audience.'

Thirty-four

Minou dressed carefully for her audience with the General. She chose a loose robe, adding a heavy lace veil to hide her face. She left aside the corset at first, then realised it might provide protection, adding a padded jacket for the same reason. Her left arm still ached from the bullet wound, but no blood was visible through the bandage. She decided to tuck the bandit's knife carefully into her boot. After all, she still had the use of her right arm to fight with.

She knew what she was about to do was a little foolish. The General would see at once she was not Ophelia. His guards would attack her, try to capture her. But she wasn't afraid. Surely the Dark Lady's protection would be with her since she'd restored the black diamond – even if she hadn't sung the final words of the hymn?

Taking a deep breath, she walked down the spiral staircase and through the maze of passages, emerging into the hall. Portraits of the General glowered from the walls, with his white-painted face and furious black eyes. A pair of gilded doors stood open, a flight of wide marble steps rising before her. Mechanical guards clanked stiffly to attention as she lowered her veil to enter the General's quarters. The yellow lamps cast a sheen around the gloomy chamber. Under the dull light, she tried to make out the figures standing there.

'By Jove!' The Commandant spoke, his ginger moustache bristling as he leaned closer. 'What is the meaning of this, Ophelia? Gallivanting in the airship with no escort. A disgrace! I realise this business with the Baron is a disappointment—'

'A disappointment? You would have preferred to see your niece marry a murderer?' Minou replied coolly.

The General, in a purple military jacket with gold buttons, started at her words. His face contorted to a grimace that cracked his white make-up into lines. With horror, Minou realised he was smiling.

'Pheelie!' She jumped as a voice screeched from beside the fireplace. 'Explain yourself, girl! Come in and shut the door.'

Minou closed the door, plunging the room further into shadow. She took a step forward. Didn't the General and his wife know she was not Ophelia?

She looked at Ophelia's mother, reclining on a chaise longue. The General's wife was ivory-skinned and red-haired like her Shadow, but with a manic glint to her eyes.

'Never mind your foolish daughter!' the Commandant harrumphed. 'I must deal with the Blacktowners. An angry mob is at the palace gates. Some foolish prophecy has led them to believe that the Queen will return when the Lally floods!'

'Brother! You ought to have tracked her down and dealt with her years ago. Didn't I warn you?' the General's wife screeched.

'She would not dare return!' The General's eyes bulged yellow against the white mask of his face.

Minou stared. How he reminded her of the old toad that sat croaking on the deck of Dima's shack, slurping insects into his mouth. She threw back her veil. 'The rightful queen is alive and has returned to Moonlally,' she announced. 'You no longer have a claim as ruler. The Dark Lady's protection has been restored to our queendom.'

'*La!* It is not Ophelia at all, but the Shadow. Guttersnipe! Cuckoo in the nest!' the General's wife cried in her parrot screech. 'Seize her!'

Minou spun, sprinting for the door and freedom, but the Commandant was upon her, gripping her elbows and squeezing her wounded arm roughly, as she kicked at his shins.

'Explain yourself!' he said through gritted teeth. 'Where is Ophelia?'

'She's with us now – with the rebels. A ruler without justice loses their kingdom day by day! Your puppet general lost his years ago – even his own daughter's against him,' Minou spat.

'What did you say?' The red-faced Commandant wrenched her arms painfully back. 'That old woman in the shack on the river, those were her words.'

Minou kicked out wildly, ignoring the agonising pain in her arm. She struggled to understand the Commandant. The old woman, did he mean Dima? Had the Commandant killed her grandmother?

'Murderer!' she gasped.

A hard slap across her face winded her. The General's wife seized her neck in a stranglehold, crushing her windpipe so she couldn't breathe 'How dare you, filthy brat? Feed her to the crocodiles like the others!'

The General was fumbling at the wall, pressing at the tiles before the fireplace. 'We must be rid of her!' he called. 'Don't let her get away...'

'Down the chute she goes!' his wife screeched.

The Commandant and the General's wife dragged Minou towards the fireplace. She buckled to the ground and tried to slide her wrists from the man's grip, arching her back to reach the hilt of the knife in her boot. Faces loomed over her and she felt the bony fingers of the General's wife tighten round her neck, digging into her throat. To her horror, she saw the back of the fireplace slide away and a yawning black space open. She kicked out desperately, trying to shake off the hands that carried her to the dark chasm. The General's white face hovered over her.

'Throw her in!' his wife screeched.

The last thing Minou saw was the glint of the General's gold buttons as she was flung head first into darkness, elbows and knees banging against the turns of a metal chute that plunged sickeningly downwards. A sour stench of fear came from the slippery walls as she slid the bumping, winding course. Minou tried to hold on – pushing out her arms, splaying her legs – anything to slow her descent, but on she tumbled, head ricocheting against the hard sides.

The knife slipped from her boot, she heard it clang down and a distant splash as it landed in the moat. *Crocodiles*, was her last thought as, bruised and sobbing, she felt her fall halted. In the darkness, she groped around to feel the knotted rope of a hammock, slung across the bottom of the chute. Gasping for breath, she called, '*Help!* Help me, please!'

A square of light appeared and hands tugged her through a narrow opening. 'Here she is! Just as I told you,' a voice said.

Pulled clear, Minou blinked at the sudden light, noise and bustle. Looking at her were the maid who'd summoned her to the General, and Jay. She'd never been more pleased to see his face.

'Sparrow! Thank the Lady you're all right! Can you stand up?' Dazed and aching all over, she was pulled to her feet. 'Quick – through this door!' Jay told her.

'Where are we?'

'The palace kitchen – but we need to get out of here – before they realise you've escaped.'

They tore outside into a blustering storm. The great court was awash, rain tumbling from skies as grey as the castle stones. A sudden crack of gunfire made them duck. Bullets whizzed past to lodge in the walls. Breaking into a run, they rounded the fortress and made for the bridge over the moat.

'*Stop!*' It was the Commandant's growl, his booted steps ringing on the path. Together, they sped on, dodging bullets until they reached the bridge. Minou jumped across in a single swift arc, throwing herself to the other side. She turned to look for Jay, who was still crossing.

'Watch out!' she screamed as the water below seethed. A huge crocodile catapulted its armoured body into the air, tail thrashing wildly. Jay stood directly in its arcing path.

Thirty-five

J ay tumbled to the floor out of the creature's way, and with a roll and a leap, cleared the bridge. Breathless, they sprinted across the great court.

'Stop there! Or I'll finish you both off – just as I did the old woman!'

Minou turned to look at the Commandant on the bridge. His pistol was aimed directly at them. 'Why did you do it – *why*?' she screamed. 'Why did you kill her?'

The old woman. He'd meant Dima, Minou knew it. She'd fired her gun at the police car, to help Tal and Little escape. And when the Commandant returned to question her, she'd told him what she thought of the General – told him straight. Dima would not back down and he had killed her for it.

The Commandant scowled and tightened his grip on the pistol.

Minou faced him, unafraid. He might have a good enough aim to hit her from where he stood, but the huge crocodile that missed Jay was still clinging to the side of the bridge. As she watched, it propelled itself on to the flat with a great thrash of its tail and moved towards the Commandant with surprising speed.

'This is the end for you, brat!' he menaced. '*Aaargh!*'

Minou flinched as the crocodile sprang, clamping its teeth over the Commandant's outstretched arm. With a harsh grunt, he fired his gun into its mouth, the beast writhing and thrashing as the bullet met its cold-blooded brain. The man staggered back and teetered on the edge of the bridge, but the locked jaws and dead weight of the animal were too much for him. His body arched into the moat, landing with a tremendous splash.

Minou watched the waters froth and redden as the other crocodiles slunk in to join the bloody feast. All at once, she found her legs would not hold her. Her arm throbbed painfully and the stink in the air – a burn of gunpowder and the taint of blood – reminded her of the day she'd found Dima. The courtyard blurred and spun. Farisht's words echoed in her head.

Two crocodiles lurk,
In a stone-hearted city.

Jay helped her to her feet, supporting her good arm. 'You're safe, Sparrow,' he told her. 'We're all safe.'

'Yes.' She blew out a breath of relief. 'How did you find me in that horrible chute?'

'The maid told Shri you'd been summoned to the General. And Little warned us about the fireplace and the crocodiles. Poor kid, he was thrown down there himself and rescued.'

Minou shuddered, remembering the face of the General, his hands pushing her into darkness. 'The chute... it leads to the moat... and the crocodiles?'

Jay grimaced. 'Unfortunately. The kitchen staff have a hammock rigged up by the feeding hatch. They rescue prisoners and help them escape. But it's not going to happen again. Look around you, Princess Sparrow. The tyrant's rule is over.'

Minou turned to see a huge crowd, assembled in the open space around the fortress. Half of Blacktown was here, waving flags painted hastily with green orchids. Some banged pots and pans, others blew whistles. Small children were hoisted up on shoulders and elders wheeled in cane chairs. She listened as their voices swelled, singing a new version of Farisht's funeral song for the General.

> *'Oh, hated General!*
> *You are a criminal.*
> *Now comes the hour,*
> *When you lose your power*
> *No longer protected – the*
> *Commandant's digested!*
> *Your end draws near*
> *Our true queen is here!'*

'Shri!' Jay pointed out. 'I think he's going to do the twenty-one-gun salute.'

They watched Shri walk into the courtyard beaming. He held up a giant purple flag with the gold elephant of Moonlally painted on it. A murmur of excitement went up from the people, as Moonlally's Magnificent Mechanical Elephant cannons were wheeled into the courtyard. Blacktowners cheered and children whooped at the sight of the great wooden creatures rumbling past, their mahogany and brass decked out with purple and gold. They trundled across the great court, water sloshing against their wheels, to form a circle around the moat.

The Commandant's carriage sped from the fortress with the General driving, his wife inside. He appeared to be in a hurry; the carriage bolted over the bridge and towards the palace gates at dangerous speed, its body rocking and wheels clattering at full tilt.

'Out of my way!' The General whipped his horses furiously as they bore down upon the crowd. '*Cockroaches!*'

'Now, boys! Take aim.' Shri lowered the flag. At his signal, a hatch in each mechanical elephant's polished flank sprang open. To Minou's astonishment, a Ragged School pupil emerged from every one.

'Faster!' The General flailed his whip as the carriage careered through the courtyard, threatening to crush anyone in its path.

'*Boom!*' Shri waved his flag again. 'And fire!'

The Ragged School boys bent to light their cannon fuses, sheltering the small flames from the rain. They leaped nimbly from the elephants, sprinting to safety as the gunpowder started to crackle and spit. The mechanical elephant trunks lifted and cannon fire resounded like thunderclaps. The horses reared, children screamed and Blacktowners ducked.

Minou laughed. The mechanical elephants, standing with their rumps to the fortress, had not fired from their trunks, but from their rear ends. They were loaded with cannonballs which clattered against the castle, leaving showers of glowing sparks. Holes pockmarked the grey stone walls, the air was thick with smoke and alarmed cries rang from the fortress as the remaining servants ducked the missiles flying towards them.

A great roar came from the people of Blacktown and the crowd parted. The Queen emerged through the haze. The General took his chance, whipping the horses wildly as the carriage made for a gap in the crowd and rattled out of the gates, his wife leaning back from the window to shake her jewelled fist.

'Let them run!' the Queen called, as she was lifted above the floodwaters and on to the roof of a palanquin. 'They won't get far.'

A hush fell as the Queen addressed her people. Somewhere in the throng, a baby cried and was comforted, but otherwise it was so quiet that Minou could hear overflowing gutters and rainwater dripping from eaves. She watched the people's entranced faces, rapt with attention, as the Queen told them how, with the Dark Lady's blessing, she had found her lost daughter. Like the Dark Lady before her, she'd returned to her queendom after thirteen years in exile. Like the

Dark Lady, she'd come with an heir, accompanied by thunder, lightning and elephants.

'As for the General,' the Queen told them. 'This means an end to his cowardice and tyranny. He'll try to save his skin but he will answer for his crimes – Moonlally is under the Dark Lady's protection once more!'

Another burst of cannon fire roared out. The walls of the General's fortress shuddered under the barrage. The boys manning the cannons cheered at the wild rejoicing of the crowd.

'Let this be a sign to those who defy their people!' The Queen raised her fist in the air. 'The Dark Lady protects us! Drive her back and her powers swell like tides with the moon. Cut her down and, like the green orchid, she flourishes on barren ground. We have seen the Lady's might in the floodwaters. But we do not fear. We will rebuild our queendom, with her blessing.'

Her mother's eyes scanned the crowd to find Minou. She raised her hand with a gentle smile. There were tears in her eyes. *Go,* her tired face seemed to say. *Do what you must. You won't be alone.*

Minou returned her mother's warm gaze. She'd seen how the Queen commanded people's hearts – but did she want such power? At the sight of her mother's kind face, her doubts faded. She had to try – she owed it to Dima.

She remembered the old shack, swaying with the rise and fall of the river. Smoke, rising from the chimney as Dima fried rice cakes for lunch. The scents of wax and palm wine as her grandmother was carried into her tomb. These memories were part of her. She would never forget where she was from, or her beloved Dima, who had raised her.

'Jay – I must go to the Dark Lady's temple.'

'Are you all right, Sparrow? Shall I come with you?'

Minou shook her head. 'Thank you. But I have to do this alone.' Slipping away unnoticed, she walked through the crumbling buildings of the old palace. 'Claudette, Gigi, Fleur!' She stopped to pet the elephants. Someone had flung open the great doors of the stables and the animals lumbered and splashed in puddles, trumpeting with joy at their unaccustomed freedom.

She pushed open the door to the temple, no longer in darkness but flooded in pale light from the Lady's third eye. Folding her hands, she kneeled in prayer, gazing in awe at the illuminated face of the goddess. *I belong here*, she thought. *This is my city.*

The Dark Lady was the goddess who guided sailors beneath the stars. She was the power of the tides lapping Moonlally's shore, the swift rush of the river, the swollen monsoon clouds. Her power was in all living things, and Minou no longer feared it. She bowed her head to chant the song of the Dark Lady.

'Dark Lady, born of the clouded hills,
whose songs summon the rains down still,
whose third eye spears in lightning strike,
whose powers turn back the highest tide.
Your radiance rivals the silver moon,

your anger brings tempest with monsoon.
Grant us blessings as pearls from oceans deep.
May your amber gaze heal those that weep.
Beloved of poets, weavers of words,
your soft voice tames wild elephant herds.
When the floodwaters rise at year thirteen,
to renew red earth and clothe her green,
then anoint our queendom's rightful queen.'

She felt the ground shudder beneath her at the final words.

'*Anoint our queendom's rightful queen,*' she whispered again, allowing the Dark Lady's power to enter her. She was part of Moonlally and the earth, water and stones of the city were part of her. She felt the toil of its farmers planting seeds, her bones rang with the hollow mines and her heart pulsed with waves breaking against its shore. She knew the people's days and nights; she felt their sorrow. One day she would be their queen.

Looking at her folded hands, Minou saw they were outlined in a faint shimmer of bluish light. She raised them to the Dark Lady. Shri had told her to ask for a boon, a wish only known to herself. What she wanted was simple. She wanted Farisht safe and back in Moonlally. Bowing, she whispered his name.

Making her way outside, she saw the purple oval of the *Napoleon* against a blackening sky. Rain had begun to fall again, thunder sounded overhead and a jagged bolt of lightning spliced the heavens. The General and his wife were attempting to escape. In their haste, they had launched the airship into a storm. It would not end well for them.

Minou watched the balloon, buffeted by turbulent winds as it flew. Lightning flashed, white lines forked closer, until the *Napoleon*'s purple silk was struck and flared fiercely, yellow flames raging. The blackening skeleton of the airship plunged through grey skies to the sea and sank slowly into its depths.

Dima's words sounded in her mind. *A ruler without justice loses his realm day by day.* The General had lost his realm and now he faced the Dark Lady's terrible justice.

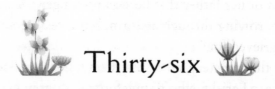

Thirty-six

Three Months Later

Dusk had fallen as Minou and her mother made their way through a crowded Blacktown Cemetery. Minou's eyes were already rimmed with red. They were here for Farisht's funeral – a funeral without a body, for despite months of searching, no trace of her friend had been found. The policemen who'd arrested him, allies of the General, had fled Moonlally once his rule was overthrown.

Earlier that day, Minou and the Queen visited the grave in Whitetown Cathedral where Tomas was buried. Minou was pleased to see the General's statue, the cause of Tal and Little's trouble, had been toppled. At Tomas's grave, Father Jacob and her mother shared memories of the father she'd never met.

'My mother,' the Queen had said, smiling at Minou, 'once warned me to be wary of Whitetowners. She said they were slippery as fishes. But Tomas was a wonderful man, kind and generous. If only he'd lived…'

Minou's heart was full of all she'd learned. Between them, Father Jacob and her mother told so many stories of her father that he was no longer a shadowy figure, rowing through a storm, but a real person she now grieved for.

At the cemetery, all of Blacktown had come to pay tribute to Farisht, who'd sung funeral songs in memory of their dead. An elderly poet had been persuaded out of retirement to sing Farisht's funeral song, his old voice wavered as his granddaughter accompanied him on a mouth organ.

> *'His words flowed like water*
> *blessed the ground like rain.*
> *Farisht means angel, but don't say*
> *he was too good for this world!*
> *A poet too good for this world*
> *deserves more than the next...'*

Candles burned at every tomb, their smoke, the sweetness of palm wine and the scent of jasmine garlands filled the cemetery air. Fireflies flitted through the dusk, hovering in flickering bursts of soft light. The Queen paused. 'I'd forgotten the fireflies,' she murmured. 'There are so many of them this year – I suppose because of the floods.'

The General and his long reign had vanished like a terrible nightmare. His grip on the city had been released and stories of injustice swept through Blacktown like the floodwaters of the Lally. Mothers spoke of lost sons, widows of missing husbands – but they were dry-eyed, for as they told the Queen, the Dark Lady had cried their tears for them.

The crowd, clutching small icons of the Lady, parted to allow Minou and the Queen to pass. Images of the Dark Lady had reappeared all over the city, made from ebony, clay or brass, placed in courtyards and at crossroads. All of Blacktown wanted to give thanks to the Dark Lady for their Queen's return.

Minou and her mother were dressed in cloth of silver, a third eye marked on their forehead in pearl dust. Minou kneeled to place a bunch of green orchids on Farisht's father's tomb, as her mother bent her head in prayer. Now the floodwaters had retreated, the rich riverside mud had rooted thousands of wildflowers and the banks of the Lally glowed bright with green orchids.

They were living with Ophelia in the old palace – the General's fortress was now an empty shell, pocked with cannon holes through which Blacktown children scavenged what they could, their possessions lost in the floods. Tents for the Blacktowners, whose homes had been destroyed, packed the courtyard and the palace cooks were kept busy feeding them. Minou hardly saw Jay, for along with Master Karu, he was organising flood relief for those affected.

Shri's small temple had become a site of pilgrimage to Blacktowners, who lined up day and night to pray to the Dark Lady, the priceless black diamond glittering from her third eye. And the crocodiles from the General's moat had been sent back to the remote swamp from where they'd once been captured.

The voices of the crowd grew stronger, singing Farisht's funeral song. Minou wanted to join in, but her throat was tight, her mouth clamped like iron. If she opened it, she would cry, not only for Farisht, or her father, but for Dima. And once she started crying, how would she stop?

She moved back to allow others to pay their respects. Ophelia stepped forward to place flowers at the grave of the poet whose words had meant so much to her. Jay smiled at her from the sea of faces.

A land that loses its stories loses its way, Farisht once told her. Could the same be true for a girl? At night, in her old bedroom, she'd wind up Shri's music box and watch the dancing figures spin and dip to the tinny music. She missed the easy camaraderie of those days on the road with Farisht, Luna the magic lantern and Laxmi the mechanical elephant. She didn't know how to behave in this new world of palaces and diplomacy, a world to which Ophelia was far more suited.

Her old story had been lost. She was no longer Dima's foundling, free to run wild in Blacktown and Whitetown alike. She was the daughter of a queen and heir to the throne – a princess – only she didn't know how to behave like one. And worse than that, she felt responsible for Farisht's death. He was her friend – why hadn't she saved him? They'd searched everywhere for him, and offered a generous reward, but he was nowhere to be found.

'What's this? What did I miss? Who's the funeral for?'

That voice – it was so familiar! Minou's heart thudded to a halt. She waited for it to beat again, blood stilling in her veins. She looked through the shifting mass of the crowd but there were too many people. She glanced at her mother, who returned her questioning look. Pushing through the mourners, she saw people turning in one direction, their attention drawn. She made her way closer, uncomfortably aware of how people bowed and murmured, 'Princess.'

Farisht! Could it really be him? She'd asked the Dark Lady for the one thing she wanted, and the Dark Lady had granted her wish.

There he was! Thinner than she remembered, dressed in the blue kilt of the hill people. A twisted pin through his earlobe replaced his gold earring, but his eyes were lined in black kohl. And he was talkative as ever, telling his story to the crowd around him.

'You won't believe what I have to say, by the Lady! The Moonlally police beat me black and blue. They threw me into a shallow grave and left me for dead. That's where the bandits found me. Robbed me of my money, but they liked my stories and so those ruffians ended up saving my life. They took me to the nuns, who cared for me until I healed – and here I am!'

'*Farisht!*' Minou screamed. The crowd parted and concerned faces turned to her.

'Sparrow!' A grin split his face in two as he stepped forward to greet her. 'And our friend Jay—'

Minou's face was wet with tears as Jay came up beside her and gave Farisht a great hug, lifting him off the ground.

'Jay – you're taller than me now! Not sure I like this,' Farisht grumbled.

Minou tried to laugh, but her laughter turned to tears. *Stop*, she told herself. *A princess doesn't cry.* She felt a hand in hers – Ophelia, who was smiling at her.

'The poet!' she whispered. 'I'm so glad.'

'Farisht – I'm sorry!' Minou told him.

'Why? Don't be sorry, this is marvellous! How many people attend their own funeral? Look at this crowd. I had no idea I was so popular. But I don't think much of the poet you hired. I'll compose my own funeral song in future—'

'Not for the *funeral*.' Minou's voice choked up with feeling. 'For leaving you!'

'But you didn't! The bandits told me of a young girl who beat their toughest men to a pulp. When I said we were friends, they couldn't have treated me better. And the nuns spoke of brave Sparrow, who fled the General's cage and flew to find her mother.'

'Why didn't you come sooner? It's been months! We had people searching for you.'

'I wanted to, but I couldn't walk and my right arm was broken. I'm not sure I'll ever sing in tune again, the amount of dirt I swallowed.'

'But you're home,' Minou whispered, squeezing Ophelia's hand and smiling at Jay. *It's over, Sparrow*, she remembered him saying. She didn't know if that was true. In a place ruled by fear for so long, the past might never be over. But her friends were together now, and together they would make things right.

Farisht echoed her thoughts. 'This is like old times – all of us here! I always say, where there's life there's hope and where there's hope, everything can begin again. Even Moonlally.'

Acknowledgements

Rohan and Leela, this book is for both of you with all my love.

I would like to thank my earliest companions on this journey: Allison DeFrees, Faye Bird, Barbara Rustin, Beverley D'Silva, Michelle Wood and Maria Waldron. Thank you for your nurturing friendship and warm encouragement.

To my Kinara sisters Sarala Estruch, Anita Pati, Shash Trevett, Rushika Wick and Sylee Gore, thank you for showing how to negotiate writing, parenting and literary citizenship with grace and indefatigable spirit.

I owe so much to the supportive and inspiring teachers of creative writing I have worked with: Anthony McGowan at Faber Academy and Michael Rosen, Julia Bell, Toby Litt & Courttia Newland at Birkbeck, University of London.

Any expression of gratitude is inadequate for the amazing Catherine Pellegrino at Marjacq who miraculously saw promise in my early work.

Thank you so much to the entirely wonderful team at Zephyr/Head of Zeus for taking this book on, especially my intuitive and meticulous editor Lauren Atherton, my copyeditor Jenny Glencross and also Megan Pickford and Fiona Kennedy.

I am eternally in debt to Mai Weitong for her beautiful illustration and to cover designer Jessie Price.

Thank you to Sabina Maharjan and Courtney Jefferies from EDPR for helping this book find its way into the world.

Most of all, thank you to my parents, Krishan and Vijay Ralleigh, especially to my mother, who by teaching me to read really began this project.

Martin, huge love and thanks for hanging on for the ride.